"You've never se

weaving?" Eva a

Jesse shook his head. "I

spare time?"

"Every moment I can find."

In his world, his old world, the women he'd hung around used their spare time to party. Suddenly, something he'd not felt in a long time rose up in him, a longing for the type of life he'd only seen on the Hallmark Channel.

Not his world.

To keep from looking at Eva, he walked over to the bookshelves and browsed the titles.

"You know, you might want to talk to my sister Elise about Timmy. She's a social worker over near Two Mules, Arizona."

"Never heard of it."

"It's small, smaller than Apache Creek. It's just a community of people trying to survive, and, according to my sister, most of them messing up."

"Messing up," he echoed. "Is that why I need to talk to her?"

Eva looked at him, her cheeks coloring.

"No, of course not. Elise deals with a lot of little kids who've had tough times. School starts next month. We need to find out if he can talk."

Jesse noticed two things then. One, though Timmy was asleep under the table again, he wasn't sucking his thumb. Two, Eva had said we.

We?

Pamela Tracy is an award-winning author who lives with her husband (…the inspiration for most of her heroes) and son (…the interference for most of her writing time). Since 1999, she has published more than twenty-five books and sold more than a million copies. She's a past RITA® Award finalist and past winner of the Christian Fiction Writers' book of the year award.

Books by Pamela Tracy

Love Inspired

Daddy for Keeps
Once Upon a Cowboy
Once Upon a Christmas

The Rancher's Daughters

Finally a Hero

Love Inspired Suspense

Pursuit of Justice
The Price of Redemption
Broken Lullaby
Fugitive Family
Clandestine Cover-Up

Visit the Author Profile page at Harlequin.com for more titles

Finally a Hero

Pamela Tracy

ISBN-13: 978-0-373-81831-0

Finally a Hero

This edition published by arrangement with Love Inspired Books.

www.Harlequin.com

Printed in U.S.A.

If anyone is in Christ, he is a new creation;
the old has gone, the new has come.

—*2 Corinthians* 5:17

To those who have learned to rise above
their circumstances, forge a new path,
and make a difference to the next generation.

Chapter One

The only thing Jesse Campbell wanted, as he stepped out of the enclosure and through the back gate of Florence State Prison, was to leave the premises, to watch the prison disappear from view, and to enjoy the sweet smell of freedom.

Forever.

Reality, however, always made its presence known.

"See you soon," said the prison guard escorting him. Five years in Florence State Prison had taught Jesse quite a bit about the system, especially when it came to the guards who played a game called "How Long Before This One Returns."

Jesse looked the man straight in the eye, something not done on the inside, and shook his head. "Not a chance."

Perspiration, tasting faintly of salt, beaded on Jesse's upper lip. The air crackled with the dryness that only a 110-degree July Arizona afternoon could provide. And as for the exhilaration that came with freedom, it disappeared before it got a toehold when Jesse looked down the walkway to the parking lot. Mike Hamm, the prison minister who'd taken Jesse under his wing, had volunteered to pick Jesse up and deliver him to his new home and job. But, two days ago, Mike's first daughter had been born a month prematurely, and he was needed elsewhere.

"No problem," Jesse had said. The prison van would take him to the bus station. The bus would drop him off in the small town of Apache Creek where he had a job lined up.

But instead of the prison van, he saw his mother standing by a broken-down, faded blue Chevy Cavalier.

He froze, unsure whether to move forward or turn back, and more than annoyed that five years in prison had taught him to wait and let someone tell him what to do.

Susan Campbell's dark hair hung past her shoulders, still long and thick. Today she wore a billowy top and tight shorts. She'd always dressed as if she were sixteen and looked as though she needed a good meal. He'd have recognized her anywhere even though he'd not seen her in seven years, two months and six days.

In prison, keeping track of dates was a favorite pastime.

Two days ago, he'd received an opened envelope with a note from his mother, their first contact in five years, two months and four days. The staff member who'd handed Jesse the envelope had raised an eyebrow while passing it over.

This note from his mother wasn't censored. Words on plain white paper proclaimed, "I'll be in touch after you get out. Got a surprise for you. S."

This was the surprise? Her coming to pick him up?

Yeah, right. She'd never been the kind of mother who understood that surprises were supposed to be good, fun, memorable. Her idea of a surprise during his early childhood had been dropping him off for an extended stay at some relative's house so she could run off and have fun with her newest boyfriend.

Back then, like the guard, she'd often said, "See you soon," and it had been Jesse playing the guessing game: how long before Mom comes back?

If ever.

The guard at Jesse's left tensed. "I thought you'd arranged for the van?"

"I did, but it's okay." The old Jesse would have said a few choice words to dear old Mom and walked away. He'd have boarded the van without giving her a chance to say a word to him. Susan had never given much of anything to him. But he wasn't the old Jesse, the angry young man who'd made a bad choice and paid the price. He was forgiven, made anew, and had the scripture from Second Corinthians to prove it: "If anyone is in Christ, he is a new creation; the old has gone, the new has come."

One of his goals as this new person was to tie up the loose ends of his life and forgive, if he could, this woman who looked older, harder, yet the same.

Susan pushed off from the car and walked toward them, stopping a few feet away when the guard held up his hand. Now Jesse could see strands of gray in her hair. "Well, you just going to stand there?" she asked.

He gripped his duffel bag more tightly. Everything he owned was inside. The bag wasn't heavy.

"You don't sound too sure," the guard said. "Is she on the list?"

"She's my mother. And, I'm not sure of anything," Jesse continued, as together they walked to meet her, "except that I don't ever want to come back to this place."

Susan hadn't moved from where she stood, but she agreed, "I'm glad to hear that. Prison's no fun."

The guard took her name, motioned her closer so he could look at her driver's license, and radioed the information in. Surprise, surprise, she was on a list Jesse didn't know existed, and yes, she could pick him up.

"Get in," she instructed him.

Every instinct warned him: *Don't do it! Run. Take the prison van.* But he'd not seen her for over seven years. Some stupid part of him still hoped she had changed. And even if she hadn't, *he* had. He was through running from his problems. From now on, he'd face them directly. He slowly followed her to the two-door car and settled his body in the passenger seat with his mostly empty duffel bag on the floorboard under his feet.

The Chevy looked like she'd been living in it with suitcases, taped boxes, dirty laundry and fast-food wrappers scattered throughout.

"Where do you want to go?" she asked, starting the engine and waving at the guard, who didn't wave back.

"Apache Creek. You need to—"

"I know where it is and how to get there."

His mother drove the way she always had, speeding toward her destination—sure that whatever was ahead improved on what she'd left behind. He fastened his seat belt and rolled the window down, not even bothering to ask about air conditioning.

Silence, an intangible accusation, accompanied them for a good five miles. Finally, Jesse couldn't take it anymore. "I'm surprised you knew I was in, much less when I was getting out."

She smiled, a tight smile that didn't reach her eyes. "I didn't, not until last week. That's when I wrote you the letter."

He didn't bother to tell her that thirteen words didn't constitute a letter. Half afraid to hear the answer, he asked, "What happened last week?"

Instead of answering, she muttered, "I hate confinement."

Jesse knew of only two times his mother had been a guest of the system. Both times he'd wound up a ward of the state.

Could he forgive her for that, and for everything else? He knew the answer should be yes...and yet he couldn't decide, not today when he had fifty bucks tucked in his sock, just the most rudimentary belongings in his duffel and the phone number of a stranger offering a job in his pocket. He was supposed to call the man at two o'clock.

He couldn't afford to blow this opportunity. If Susan ruined it for him, as she'd ruined so many things in the past, then that would be a real challenge even for a Christian to forgive.

As they sped down the highway, he took note of his surroundings. It had been, after all, over five years since his view wasn't obstructed by a chain-link fence. The scenery wasn't much to brag about. To his right was a giant parking area waiting for winter when a flock of snowbirds in RVs would descend. To the left was the empty shell used by the Renaissance fair in the winter. Neither landmark welcomed him to sweet freedom.

Both were better than prison.

"What happened last week?" he finally asked again. "Does it have to do with the surprise you wrote about?"

She didn't answer. Instead, she nodded toward an interstate sign announcing Apache Creek Next Exit and left the highway. As she slowed the car, she looked in the rearview mirror, at the suitcases, boxes and clothes scattered in the back. He'd seen that expression on her face many a time. She felt trapped, like life had passed her by and somehow she'd missed out on what she deserved.

"I had a ride," he said. "You didn't need to pick me up."

"Yes, I did." She drove down the main drag, slowing when she passed a fast-food restaurant, then a bar and grill, before finally turning into the parking lot of a rustic café. "You hungry?"

He doubted he could swallow a bite. For the past hour, he'd been trapped in a car with the mother he needed to forgive. The whole hour had felt eerily like still being in jail: trapped, at someone else's mercy.

If anyone is in Christ, he is a new creation; the old has gone, the new has come.

He'd eat with her, forgive her and walk away knowing he'd done the right thing. "I'm a bit hungry."

She parked close to the front door. Jesse grabbed his duffel and exited the car. He had the address for his new job in his pocket; he'd get directions and walk from here. He didn't care how hot it was. Walking would still be better than getting a ride from Susan, letting her know where to find him if she wanted to drag him into her troubles again. He stepped back, watching his toes, as a big blue pickup truck pulled in next to them. A curvy blonde, playing country music loud enough for him to sing along, turned off the engine, opened her door and climbed down.

She smiled, the half-shy expression of someone who knew how to be polite. Then she hurried around them and toward the front door of the Miner's Lamp Café.

His mother hesitated for the first time, acting almost insecure. "I need to introduce you to someone." He looked at the restaurant, noticing the blonde still watching him. His mother, however, wasn't looking at the woman. His mother's gaze centered on one spot in the cluttered backseat, and Jesse leaned in to see what had her so distracted.

What Jesse had mistaken for dirty laundry was anything but. Now he saw the end of one bare foot sticking out from old jeans too big for the boy's small frame. Then came a dirty T-shirt advertising a rock group no child that age should know about.

"Timmy, wake up!"

A small head rose with dark-brown hair—the same color as Jesse's—badly in need of a wash. The boy's thumb was in his mouth. Sweat trickled down his cheek, looking like a teardrop.

Suddenly Jesse couldn't swallow. There was a huge lump in his throat, and it hurt.

This was him twenty-odd years ago, maybe five years old. Had his mother—?

"Meet your son," his mother said.

Eva Hubrecht tried not to listen, tried to hurry into the restaurant without disturbing the man and woman in the blue car. They were obviously in crisis, and with everything that was going on in her own life, she couldn't handle one more.

Turning the corner, she overheard the woman say, "Really, this is your son. His name is Timmy."

Eva didn't stop to hear what the man said next. It would keep her awake at night. Make her think that losing next week's wedding party, accounting for half the ranch's July reservations, wasn't the worst thing that could happen to someone after all.

The wedding had been called off entirely, and because the couple had canceled more than forty-eight hours in advance, Eva now had six empty rooms, three empty suites, two empty cabins and not even a hefty cancellation fee to make up for the lost revenue.

It was a seven-thousand-dollar loss, during the summer, when they could least afford it.

She allowed the restaurant door to slam behind her, didn't wait for the hostess, and instead headed for her favorite booth. Her ultimate goal had been to settle into a booth, bemoan her bad luck to the waitress, her best friend Jane de la Rosa, and maybe lose herself in a paperback.

Now she felt even more unsettled, questioned just how bad her luck was and doubted she'd be able to read past a paragraph.

What had she just witnessed? Possibly a family more dysfunctional than hers?

"Hey, girlfriend." Jane set an iced tea in front of Eva. "Tell me, did you do it?"

Eva knew exactly what Jane was talking about. "No. I made it all the way to the stable, walked to Snow White's stall and actually aimed my hand for her nose."

"Then?"

"Then, Pistol let out a loud snort and did a dance in the next stall." Finally Eva admitted, "I ran."

"Anyone see?"

"I'm pretty sure Harold was in the tack room. But he didn't look out, laugh or say anything. Last week he offered to help me on Snow White's back and walk me around the arena. But I don't want to feel like I'm eight years old, needing someone to hold my hand before I can deal with a horse. And I don't want to fail in front of anyone, especially not my dad."

"Nothing wrong with being eight years old," Jane said. "Sometimes you need to start where you left off. And the only failure is not trying."

Then, without writing a single word on her order pad, Jane stuck it in her apron pocket and said, "I already told the kitchen you were here. They started your meal. So, you look to be in a mood. Something else happening at home?"

"No, something happening in your parking lot. Just a strange family..." Eva let her words taper off. It really wasn't any of her business. "...Having some, er, difficulties."

"I'm sorry I had to cancel our movie tonight," Jane said, not even blinking at the thought of a strange family outside. Eva figured she probably saw plenty of odd people passing through town. The Miner's Lamp Café was one of the few sit-down restaurants between Phoenix and Florence.

"I need the extra shift money," Jane continued. "Did you ask someone else to go with you?"

Eva shook her head.

"You know, Sam Miller would love to go to the movies with you," Jane said. "If you go with him, my mother would stop nudging me in his direction."

That both Eva and Jane were single put them at the top of Jane's mom's to-do list. Sam was the only single guy at their church who fit Patti de la Rosa's fit-for-my-daughter criteria list: age-appropriate, employed and Christian. That he was also a high school friend and a cop worked in his favor.

Jane's mother was a full-time employee on the Lost Dutchman Ranch and had been offering Eva's dad parenting advice since Eva was in grade school, thus her name on a wish list. Patti claimed that neither of the girls got out enough and seemed to see it as her job to fix that.

"No, not interested," Eva said. "Dad's got a new ranch hand coming in today, and I want to be there. Something's going on, and I can't quite put my finger on it."

"What do you mean?"

"Dad's being secretive, more so than usual. Makes me worry. Last time we brought in a new hire this quickly, it was Mitch."

Jane made a face. "I remember. Last summer he was the one who wanted to sleep until noon every day and then needed two hours before he was ready to work. You hired him back, right?"

"Dad did. And the time before that it was some writer who wanted to work on the ranch as research for his book. We actually needed someone in that position. He quit the second day, muttering about dirty fingernails and finding a scorpion in his boot."

"I hate when my fingernails get dirty," Jane joked.

"Yeah." Eva looked at her own nails. Unpainted, cut short, but very clean. Then she studied her hands, smooth and soft—without the calluses she'd have if she could find the courage to get back in the saddle. "We certainly can't afford a new hand, especially now. But Dad just says yes to anyone who asks."

"Your busy season's coming up in a month or two. Maybe your dad's thinking ahead."

"Maybe," Eva said, but she didn't believe it. Her dad had a weakness for hard-luck cases and a habit of taking in ex-alcoholics, ex-cons and ex-rodeoers. Sometimes the ex-rodeoers worked out.

A bell sounded from the kitchen. Jane headed for the back with an "I'll be right out with your meal."

The moment Jane disappeared, the restaurant's door opened. Eva reached down, snagged her book from her purse and randomly turned to a page as she tried to ignore the family. It wasn't easy. They were the elephant in the room, and fact was much more entertaining than fiction.

The woman was loud and defensive. She kept prodding the little boy forward. "Hurry up, Timmy. Sit down, Timmy." Once the kid was settled, she dropped her car keys on the table with a clatter. The man wore brand-new jeans, about two sizes too big, and a dark-blue T-shirt that stretched across his chest. He looked like he'd rather be anywhere else. Well, from what Eva had overheard, no wonder. He slid a duffel bag under the table and put his left foot on it as if he were afraid it would escape. His gaze slid across the room, finding hers and locking in. His eyes were dark and brooding. The little boy looked in need of a bath and scared of both adults.

Embarrassed, Eva turned away. Her youngest sister, Emily, would see a story begging to be told. Eva just saw people struggling with problems they'd made for themselves and probably did nothing to change.

"Here ya go," Jane said, putting a hot plate in front of Eva and snagging ketchup and maple syrup from her apron pocket. "Your toast will be out in a few minutes. Cook burnt it."

"That's okay. You've got some other customers." Eva nodded at the newcomers.

"Oh, thanks. I didn't hear them come in." Jane took out her pad and headed over to stand between the man and boy.

The little boy was eating a cracker left on the table from a previous diner. His dirty, bare feet were tucked under him as if he knew that shoes were required.

"I'm hungry, haven't eaten since last night," the woman said, then loudly gave her order and the boy's. Once the man made his selection and Jane walked away, the man leaned in to do the talking.

"I can't believe you didn't call me, didn't put this in the letter," the man said, obviously trying to keep his voice low.

Maybe Eva should just leave. When Jane came back, Eva'd ask for a to-go box, never mind the toast.

"Surprise for me, too," the woman insisted. "This Matilda showed up at my house last Monday. She said she couldn't take care of Timmy anymore. She showed me his birth certificate. Your name isn't on it, but look at the kid. He's you all over again."

Eva peeked over her book. Same hair, same facial shape, same skin tone, same deer-in-the-headlights expression. Yup, they were related.

Just then Jane brought out salads for their table. The moment she finished, Eva would let her know she needed a to-go box. The woman dug right in. So did the boy. The man, however, bowed his head in prayer.

Something Eva had forgotten to do.

She'd been too busy being judgmental.

Chapter Two

It didn't seem possible, but the longer Jesse stared at the boy, the more he believed it. He had a son.

He tried to think of a scripture where a surprise son or daughter appeared, but couldn't. Joseph might have been surprised when Mary told him about the son she carried, but she'd not followed the pronouncement with "Guess what? He's yours."

"So, you met Matilda?" It was all he could think of to say.

"Interesting girl," his mother said.

Jesse'd lived with Matilda Scott for three months, just after he'd aged out of the foster system. He'd managed to deal with the assigned group home for only three days. Matilda's one-room apartment had been an oasis for the next few months. Then she'd disappeared overnight, leaving him with rent due and a vague fear that he'd just been used by a woman too much like his mother.

He'd steered clear of relationships ever since.

Easy enough, since he'd spent much of that time in prison.

"But then, I only talked with her for all of twenty minutes." His mother shook her head, her expression half mad, half impressed. "She knocked on the door. Next thing I knew, she was in the house telling me that Timmy was your son and that she had dreams to pursue. She wanted me to keep Timmy until you got out of prison. She kept saying, 'It's just nine days.' I told her no. I mean, come on. Couldn't she see we were in a one-bedroom apartment? She went to use the restroom and crawled out the window and disappeared. Wonder what she would have done if I hadn't been on the first floor? And, she left me with the kid! If I'd been sober, she wouldn't have gotten away with it."

Looking across the table at Timmy, he tried to decipher if the young boy showed any emotion at being abandoned. Not really. Then, Jesse looked at his mother and tried to see any hint of interest, grandparental pride, something.

Nothing.

"How'd Matilda find you?"

"Didn't get around to asking," Susan said. "And she didn't bother telling."

"Timmy," Jesse said, "did you know Matilda, your mom, planned on dropping you off?"

The yellow crayon clutched between Timmy's

fingers was quickly becoming a nub. The little boy didn't look from the gold-panning scene he was coloring.

"Do you know your mom's phone number?" Jesse tried next.

"I've already asked him, at least twice a day. He hasn't said a word. I don't think he can talk. Anyway, she didn't leave a phone number or previous address. Nothing except her car, some games and a bunch of clothes." His mother picked up her fork and ate her food as if it had been a week since her last meal. She didn't look at Timmy.

He'd felt that same parental disconnect during his childhood. Felt it now, at twenty-four years of age. He didn't know the woman sitting across from him, felt no connection. When Jesse was very young, he hadn't been allowed to call her "mother." She'd passed him off as her younger brother because calling him her son might have discouraged boyfriends. The deception worked for a little while because she'd had him at fifteen. But as time passed, the drugs and hard living made her look even older than her actual age.

Matilda had dropped off their son and disappeared? Jesse had no history, nothing to go on. Where had they been living? Had Matilda tried to be a good mom? What had happened? He had all kinds of questions, but they were not ones he'd ask in front of the child. Already, though, he knew his mother was telling the truth. Matilda had abandoned Timmy the same way Matilda had abandoned Jesse. And the same way Jesse's mother used to abandon him.

This wasn't how he'd pictured his first day of freedom. Jesse wanted to come to town, meet his employer and join productive society: the working world. He needed time to figure out his future.

He'd need a lifetime to figure out what to do with Timmy.

"You need to eat," his mother advised him. "I, for one, am starved."

Any appetite Jesse might have had disappeared with the words "Meet your son."

The waitress, way too happy, came over and refilled Jesse's water glass. She scooted Timmy's milk glass closer to him as if to hint "Drink this. It does a body good." If she noticed something amiss, she didn't let it show.

She walked away from them to chat with the blonde seated in the corner. When Jesse looked over, he noticed the woman was watching him, her expression guarded and somewhat disdainful. He got the feeling she knew not only where he came from and what he'd done but had already made up her mind that his future would be just as bleak. The look on her face was the same one the guard had given him before saying he'd see him soon. Yet for all that, she was a pretty thing, all long blond hair and Westerny: clean and soft.

Clean and *soft* weren't the words most females wanted to hear, but to a man fresh out of prison, they were powerful. She looked like someone well taken care of.

Someone smart enough to stay away from him.

Her cheeks colored about the time Jesse looked away. He had other things to focus on, like a newly discovered son.

He took the first bite of his hamburger, washing it down with a swig of water, and asked, "Did Matilda say why she dropped Timmy off? Was she in some kind of trouble? I mean, did she say when she'd be back?"

His mother rolled her eyes. "She didn't even say she was leaving before she climbed out the bathroom window without taking her kid."

Timmy didn't act like he knew they were talking about him.

"And, you've had him how long?" Jesse asked.

"Nine days now."

Jesse figured in those nine days, his mother had done more talking *at* the kid than *to* the kid. That was her style. Looking at Timmy, she said, "His mother left a twenty, but that didn't last long. I've had to buy lots of extra food, stuff I normally don't buy. Things like spaghetti, peanut butter, jelly and Pop-Tarts. Nothing in the car worth selling.

Believe me, I looked. And then there's the gas for driving him here."

He knew exactly what his mother was telling him and took a deep breath. She wanted to be reimbursed. But what money could she honestly expect from a man who'd been out of jail for only a few hours? He was living on faith, but had no clue how faith could help Matilda, his mother or Timmy. Part of him wanted to pray; part of him wanted to run out of the restaurant. Instead, hating himself for what he couldn't provide, he said, "You've come to the wrong man. Right now, I can barely help myself."

"Not sure you'll have a choice."

If not for the generosity of Mike Hamm, he wouldn't even have the clothes on his back. The prison chaplain had provided him with the pants and shirt, not wanting him to leave prison in state-provided denim blues.

"I don't have anything to give," he told his mother.

She didn't respond. Instead, resignation on her face, she glanced out the restaurant window, looking like she wished she was miles away. He knew she wasn't wishing to be any place in particular—just anywhere but where she was.

The boy watched, not uttering a word, ignoring Jesse's attempts to ask him about age, school status and favorite things to do. The yellow crayon broke, and now Timmy colored with a dark blue crayon.

"Got a job lined up?" his mother finally asked after checking her watch for a third time.

"Yes."

Susan gave a shrug and took the last bite of her meal. "That's more than I can manage. Soon, though, things will be better. I've met a guy, a nice guy, and we're heading for New Mexico. Maybe this time it will last."

Jesse had never figured out what the "it" his mother talked about was. When he was young, he'd thought it meant love. As a teenager, he'd thought it meant monetary support. Now, as an ex-con, he figured it meant companionship and money.

His mother didn't really understand the concept of love, so that couldn't be it.

"He's not crazy about the kid, I'll tell you that," Susan continued. As if cued, her cell phone sounded a rendition of "Free Bird." She picked it up and looked at the number. "Oh, it's him." She answered with a "Hey," then stood and said to Jesse, "Let me take this where I can hear."

She headed to the front of the restaurant and stopped at the door. Before exiting, she said, "He'll be excited that you and I met up."

Somehow Jesse doubted it. In all his years, not one of Susan's boyfriends had been excited about meeting Jesse. And certainly, meeting Jesse—fresh out of prison—with Timmy as collateral damage was more than any significant other could take.

Jesse turned his attention back to his meal. The food was better than anything he'd had in the past few years and he intended to enjoy it while he could—and enjoy the momentary silence before his mother returned.

Working at the ranch, being in charge of guest relations, Eva'd seen dysfunctional families up close and personal. As a matter of fact, she'd called the police a time or two, and once drove a woman all the way to California when her husband decided to end their marriage in the middle of their vacation.

Not fun.

She wasn't sure how the woman who'd just sashayed from the restaurant was connected to Timmy's father. He'd never spoken to her by name. She dressed young, but her face bore the lines of hard living. She'd introduced the boy as "your son" and not "our son."

The man, on the other hand, didn't look as rough—in part because he clearly had God in his life. Again, Eva felt a nudge of guilt. Last Sunday morning's sermon had been about being judgmental. Sitting beside her father on the pew, Eva knew this was a trait she struggled with. At the front desk of the ranch, she often decided on personalities of people before they'd finished check-in.

She judged which parents were too easy on their offspring. She judged which family would prove to be good tippers and which would leave their rooms an absolute mess. She was often right—but she'd been wrong a time or two.

Maybe she'd misjudged the man across the restaurant.

Eva glanced out the window and watched as the woman passed the bench by the front door, quickly lit up a cigarette, and then headed alongside the building.

The phone call must be really private for her to go out back where the Dumpsters were located. Except...she'd already put away her phone.

Stop it, Eva told herself. *This is ridiculous. Go back to your book.* She reread the last paragraph, but she'd forgotten the storyline.

Outside, the woman walked up to a man on a motorcycle.

Feeling slightly ridiculous, Eva glared at the doors to the kitchen. The bill...Eva really needed her bill. She was worried, actually worried about the two males left behind. And she didn't even know them! If the restaurant hadn't been so empty and the family—at least the woman—so noisy, Eva wouldn't be so curious.

At least curiosity wasn't a sin.

Not in moderation.

The rev of the motorcycle engine sounded right outside. Eva sighed and gave up pretending that she wasn't watching. Peering through the window, Eva watched as the woman took one last puff from a cigarette before throwing it to the ground. She seemed agitated.

She also seemed to know the man on the motorcycle. Well enough that she climbed on the seat and wrapped her arms around his leather jacket. And then, off they went.

Eva hoped she hadn't just witnessed someone getting dumped, especially not a someone who'd just heard the words "Meet your son."

None of my business, Eva reminded herself.

But she knew the woman hadn't said goodbye. And she knew what it was like to wait for someone who had no intention of returning.

She glanced back at the two guys left in the restaurant. The little boy, Timmy, picked at his food, eating with his fingers, and making a mess of his face. The man pushed an extra napkin in his direction, but Timmy ignored it, coloring more vigorously in between bites of food. Then his crayon rolled toward the edge of the table, and when he moved to grab it, he knocked over his water glass. Water covered the page he'd been coloring. Timmy froze.

Eva knew that response. The kid expected some kind of punishment.

"It's okay," the man said, gently. "We've got plenty of napkins."

Just then, Jane showed up with more. Timmy was an unyielding mannequin. He looked like he was barely breathing. The man literally had to scoot the boy's chair out of the way so Jane could clean the table.

Eva looked out the window again. The motorcycle and its two riders were long gone.

Jane brought Timmy a new coloring sheet. "You want dessert?" she asked.

"No, my mother stepped outside to take a call," the man said. "As soon as she returns, we'll pay the bill and take off."

So the woman was his mother. But if he waited for her to come back, they'd be waiting a long time. Eva waved Jane over.

"You need to tell him," Eva whispered, "that his mother just took off on a motorcycle with some guy."

Jane took a step back. "You're kidding. I don't want to tell him."

"We can't leave them waiting."

"You tell him," Jane said, and before Eva could stop her, she'd motioned for him to join them.

Eva watched as he glanced at his mother's keys,

at Timmy and then at the front door before joining them.

Eva should have left a twenty on the table and hightailed it from the restaurant. Then she wouldn't have been in this uncomfortable position. She looked out the window again, hoping the woman would magically appear. "You're waiting for your friend to come back?"

"My mother," the man admitted, then leaned forward, one strong hand braced on Eva's table and the other pushing the curtain farther aside. "Did she fall or something?"

"Um," Eva said, "I think she took off with some man on a motorcycle. I couldn't see his face because he wore a helmet. They took off down the road, probably toward the interstate."

"Oh, man, you've got to be kidding." He'd had a stoic, too-serious expression from the time they'd entered the restaurant, but now she could clearly read shock all over his face.

Eva shook her head, not kidding.

He marched over to his table and ordered Timmy, "Stay here. I'll be right back."

The boy didn't move. Hadn't since he'd spilled his water. But once his father turned away from him, he started edging to the floor and under the table.

As Eva and Jane watched, the man stepped outside, looked to the right and left. Not much happening on this blistering August day. It was after the noon rush, and the parking lot was empty save for four cars, including the one Eva had watched him arrive in.

Then he came back inside. Timmy was completely under the table, thumb in mouth, beginning a curious humming sound. The man walked past him, straight for Eva. "Tell me what you saw," he ordered.

"I saw her leaving."

"Story of my life," he muttered.

Chapter Three

He must have quite a story, but Eva didn't want to know what happened in the next chapter. She liked her days to run smoothly. She'd spent her whole life, it seemed, trying to make sure the people around her were happy and that everything was in its place.

Sometimes she succeeded.

The past hour left her feeling worried and disgruntled. She exited the restaurant and climbed into the royal-blue Ford F-250 pickup decorated with the logo and phone number for the Lost Dutchman Ranch.

Driving out of Apache Creek township and into the rural area where the ranch waited, Eva remembered every detail from the restaurant. The man had obviously just had a son dropped in his lap by a mother who wasn't much of a mother—or grandmother, apparently. Eva couldn't even fathom the type of woman who'd sneak out of a restaurant leaving family behind not knowing.

She wondered how the man would get Timmy out from under the table. She had never been around reticent children. Her sisters had never been afraid to show their feelings.

She didn't remember fear being part of her childhood—not fear of people, anyway. Fear of horses was a whole different story. The worst thing, the thing that made the Hubrecht clan dysfunctional, was her dad's habit of thinking he always knew best, and that his word was law, to be followed without question. But he'd never made them feel like they should be afraid. He'd never raised a hand to them. His punishment was "You're grounded. No television or horse privileges for a week." And under all the bluster was a heart made of gold. Eva saw it even if her sisters didn't.

But Timmy was afraid.

Eva could only wonder what would happen to the boy now that the man had been left in possession of his son. And she couldn't quite shake the connection she'd felt with the man the first time his gaze had caught hers. There was something about him that made her want to get involved. But no, she'd held the enabler card before, and it never played well for her.

And this time, she hadn't even gotten the name of the man who caused her such angst.

Pulling into the Lost Dutchman Ranch, she finally relaxed. She felt like she'd already put in a full day, though it was just past lunchtime. No way could she be a social worker like her sister Elise. Her small involvement with the people at the restaurant had totally drained her.

"We have nothing to complain about," she announced to Patti de la Rosa, Jane's mom, as she entered the lobby and headed for the front desk.

"I told you that a long time ago. Jane just called and told me all about what happened at the restaurant. Poor man. Jane says he's still there trying to get his son to come out from under the table. I'm going to add him to the prayer list at church."

Eva sat down behind the front desk and checked the answering machine and their website.

"You don't want to do that," Patti advised her. "It'll just depress you." As office assistant and head of housekeeping, Patti knew everything there was to know about the workings of the Lost Dutchman. "I already put up the cancellation specials. Not even ten minutes passed before a family called in, canceled their original reservation and hung up. Then, five minutes later, they called and re-reserved under the special price, this time using the husband's name and card."

Eva closed her eyes. When a block of rooms suddenly opened up, it was good policy to offer last-minute price breaks to potential guests who might be looking for spur-of-the-moment deals.

Today it hadn't worked in the ranch's favor.

"We did get two bookings for October," Patti said helpfully.

October filled no matter what. Snowbirds flocked to Arizona for its perfect weather.

"I was really hoping for a good summer season," Eva said. "I need to go find Dad and tell him we can't afford this new hire. We can't." She checked the dining hall, the kitchen and her dad's office. He wasn't in their living areas. Standing on the back porch, she looked down the desert landscaping and toward the barn. That's where he'd be.

She had a love/hate relationship with the barn. On one hand, she hated the way it made her feel: scared, trapped, inadequate. On the other, she came from a long line of horsemen and very much wanted to join their ranks.

She wanted to ride with her dad, her sisters, her someday children.

Go down there, she told herself. *You're a grown woman, strong, and you manage the Lost Dutchman. All of it.*

Her feet obeyed, and one step at a time, she walked the half mile to the barn. She could have hopped on one of the ranch's all terrain vehicles, but that would have gotten her there sooner. She'd face the barn when she got there, but she wasn't exactly in a rush to make that happen.

She found her father in the saddle room, mending a hobble strap. Chris LeDoux played on the radio.

"You gonna tell me what's going on, Dad? Do we really need another hand?"

Jacob Hubrecht still had a full head of hair, light brown and brushed to the side. His eyebrows were bushy, his mouth wide. Age had given him wrinkles, very defined, but he still looked strong, and had certainly held on to all his stubbornness through the years. He didn't pause in his task. "I know what I'm doing. I've got the good of the ranch in mind. Leave it be."

Her two younger sisters had rebelled against his unyielding authority. Eva, however, usually understood where her father was coming from and agreed. Not this time, though.

She didn't move, just stared at him.

"I'm not getting any younger," he finally said. "It's time to put some new, young, strong employees into place—" his hands, always so capable, formed into fists "—so that when I need to work less, I can know all is being cared for."

He had to be talking about the horses because Eva could do everything else.

She *wanted* to do everything. Then he wouldn't be hiring a hand they couldn't afford.

Behind her, a horse snorted as if reading her mind and knowing she couldn't possibly care for the mares and geldings like her father did.

"So, this new guy is permanent?"

"Probably not. Mike Hamm called and asked for a favor."

Mike Hamm was the prison minister. Yes, this was an example of her father not being able to say no to another hard-luck case.

And deep down, she knew he was thinking, "I have three beautiful daughters, but I needed to have me a boy."

Well, Eva could shoot as well as any boy. Her younger sister Elise could ride like a boy. And the baby of the family, Emily, was a master with a hammer and nails. Half the fences on the ranch were still standing because of Emily. As a matter of fact, Emily had helped Dad draw the plans for most of the Lost Dutchman's lodgings.

Eva shifted nervously on her feet, all too aware of the two ailing horses in the barn who restlessly watched her. One had stepped on a muck rake and suffered a gash near her eye. Dad was keeping her under observation for a day or two. The other had a dislocated ankle. His future looked grim.

Eva was no help at all. The sight of blood made her woozy, and the thought of trying to help hold a horse while a vet or some of the hands examined it made her. . .yup, just as woozy.

She'd owned fifty plastic horses as a preteen. She'd had posters of horses on her wall. She'd read *Black Beauty* and all the Walter Farley books twenty times. Yet the real McCoy, an actual horse, scared her to death.

Daisy, the horse with the gash, snorted again.

Her dad continued. "I know he needs a job. I know he moved a lot and was in foster care. He needs a place to set down roots. Mike says he worked at horse camps during a few summers and remembers the time as the best in his life."

Great, she was being replaced by a city slicker who only had to muck stalls for two and a half months a few summers.

"I don't like this change—" Eva had more to say, but Waylon Jennings and Willie Nelson's "Mammas, Don't Let Your Babies Grow Up to Be Cowboys" started playing. Her father pulled his cell from his back pocket and answered, "Hubrecht."

As she walked away, she could hear him saying, "Yeah, I've been expecting your call."

And wasn't that typical. With a stranger, some shiftless criminal he'd never even met, her father was all expectation. But he had no expectations for her.

Just disappointment.

Jesse gathered up every crumb left over from lunch and loaded the food into a doggy bag. The monotonous task gave him time to think about what on earth he was going to do now that he had his son in his care.

He'd spent about twenty minutes on the waitress's cell phone, calling his parole officer and Mike Hamm to update them on his situation. The parole officer gave him an emergency appointment for tomorrow. Mike Hamm's voice mail promised only that Mike considered the call important and would return it as soon as possible.

Jesse knew no other people's phone numbers, except for the man offering him a job. Taking the keys from the table, Jesse paid the check—twenty dollars gone. Then he tried to get Timmy out from under the table for the second time.

Timmy was happy under the table.

It took another thirty minutes and a dish of ice cream, but finally he hustled Timmy out the door and toward the old Chevy. At least his mother, or really Matilda, had left something substantial behind. Maybe he could sell it.

Good thing his mother hadn't thought of that.

A quick search through the backseat showed that the suitcases and dirty laundry were all Timmy's. The half-full boxes contained old games and toys. Not one item in the car belonged to Susan.

Timothy Leroy Scott's birth certificate was in an envelope in the glove box. Matilda's name was in the box labeled Mother, but no name was listed for Father. Jesse did the math. Timmy would be five and yes, he'd been with Matilda during the time she'd conceived Timmy.

He reminded himself to be glad his mother had gotten more organized. When she'd dumped Jesse with relatives, sometimes school wasn't an option because he never arrived with a birth certificate.

Maybe that's why he'd never finished high school—too far behind and too busy trying to survive.

"This car belong to your mother?" Jesse asked.

Timmy stared at the ground.

"What am I going to do with you?" Jesse asked.

Timmy didn't move, not an inch.

"Has Matilda—has your mother—left you before?"

Finally a vague response, a slight shake of the head. At least, Jesse thought it was a shake. It could have been the kid simply needed to get his hair out of his eyes.

"Well, get in."

Timmy started to climb in back, but Jesse said, "No, the front's okay."

The Chevy started on the third try. The radio refused to turn on. Come to find out, the air conditioner didn't work. Jesse had no sooner pulled onto the street than the rearview mirror fell off.

"Great," Jesse said, tossing it in the backseat with the rest of the junk.

The prison minister would be proud. Since leaving jail this morning, Jesse'd been maneuvering around unexpected roadblocks one right after another, and there'd been not a curse word uttered. His tongue was bleeding a little from where he'd bitten it too hard, but still...progress.

Timmy didn't say anything, just looked from the space where the rearview mirror should have been to Jesse as if expecting to get blamed.

"It will be all right," Jesse assured the boy. "My mother did the same thing to me many times, and believe me, many a day I felt as conflicted as you probably do right now."

Timmy gave the barest of shrugs and concentrated on whatever he could see from the window. There wasn't much. Apache Creek was one long street of businesses, most looking fairly deserted. There were homes to the north and the freeway and hotels to the south. East and west were desert and a smattering of homes.

The main color was brown.

Checking his watch, Jesse groaned. It was now almost two. He needed to call the man offering him a job.

A job.

Right. Could be that opportunity was a thing of the past, given his new circumstances. Jesse was supposed to be a single man intent on getting his life back together. Instead—for the next few days, anyway—he'd be a man who had no clue what to do, especially not with a kid.

And no money.

Maybe he could get on the internet and find some of those long-lost relatives who'd taken him in when Susan disappeared on some misguided quest for happiness.

No, the best had merely tolerated him.

The worst had…

No way could Jesse turn over to them a five-year-old who flinched after spilling a glass of water and who hid under tables.

He had to get this job.

The first convenience store didn't have a pay phone. The second one didn't either, but the girl behind the counter handed over her cell and said, "Go ahead, man. Just don't leave the store."

Jesse motioned Timmy toward the candy aisle. Good, something sparked the kid's interest. Then, Jesse pulled out the folded, wrinkled paper from his back pocket. For the past week, he'd stared at the name penciled on the paper every day, thinking about opportunities and fresh starts.

And freedom.

He punched in the number and after just one ring heard, "Hubrecht."

"Yes, hello, sir…" Jesse cleared his throat and started again because gravelly wasn't the tone he was going for. “Yes, hello, my name is Jesse Campbell and—”

“Yeah, I’ve been expecting your call. Where are you?”

Glancing at the sign outside, Jesse said, “A Circle K next to a Burger King right on what looks to be the main street.”

“I’ll come get you.”

“I have a vehicle. I can meet you if that’s easier.”

“Good. There’s a restaurant just down the way, the Miner’s Lamp Café and—”

“I just ate lunch there.” No way did Jesse want to return. “Look, there’s a park across the street. I can see some picnic tables.”

“It will take me about twenty minutes,” Jacob said.

“Thank you.” Jesse handed the phone back to the girl, grabbed two bottled waters from the case, and then paid for them and a candy bar for Timmy.

Jesse noticed that Timmy waited until he thought Jesse wasn’t looking and put the candy bar in one of his pockets.

Jesse’d done that a time or two also, saving food for later in case mealtimes became sporadic or nonexistent.

“It will melt,” Jesse told him. Then he handed Timmy a dollar. “Go ahead and enjoy your candy bar. If you find you need another one later, you can buy one. Never steal.”

Never steal, never steal, never steal.

Timmy took the money and put it in the pocket with the candy bar, which he still made no move to eat.

Wherever Susan and Timmy had been, it must not have been Arizona in July. Well, based all on the things that had gone wrong today, a little melted chocolate would be the easiest to fix.

There were two boys already at the park, both older than Timmy. They didn't really play on the equipment. They were more interested in chasing, pushing each other to the ground and roughhousing. Timmy didn't even look at them. Instead, he sat in the sand, found an old plastic spoon and began digging.

Jesse watched him, wondering what on earth he was going to do with a kid. At this moment, he wasn't sure if he even remembered how to take care of himself. One thing about prison—you were told what to do and when to do it, and knew the consequences if you got caught not complying.

Tomorrow Jesse needed to drive into Phoenix and meet his parole officer. Now that would be fun. Good old Child Protective Services would get involved, and one more government organization would be breathing down Jesse's neck.

If they didn't take Timmy away entirely. He already dreaded the thought of each and every hoop he'd need to jump through.

July in Arizona was unrelenting. The heat pressed down, and Jesse felt sweat trickling over his shoulder blades. Timmy didn't seem to notice or care. The plastic spoon broke. Timmy left it where it was and dug with his hands instead. He looked like he was on a mission.

Maybe he wanted to escape.

Jesse could sympathize with the sentiment, but after five years of confinement, Jesse found that finally being in a wide-open space was so overwhelming, he couldn't breathe.

Everything he'd dreamed for the past few months was shattering around him. He'd left prison with a set of goals cemented in his mind, and already those goals were being either erased or challenged.

He wasn't sure he was strong enough to make new ones or even battle for the old ones.

No, he couldn't think that way. He'd come too far.

But, really, Jesse couldn't think of a worse day to gain a son, especially a son who didn't talk.

"You thirsty?" Jesse asked.

Timmy ignored him.

Jesse thought back to the past three months. He'd kept waiting for someone to say, "There's been a mistake. You won't be paroled." When he'd asked Mike Hamm for a scripture, Mike had turned to Joshua: "Have I not commanded you? Be strong and courageous. Do not be terrified; do not be discouraged, for the Lord your God will be with you wherever you go."

Amazing how a few words from God could help.

Amazing how they'd helped more during incarceration than now.

The street remained empty. Everyone was at work or at home in the air conditioning. Even the little boys who were wrestling had reached their limit and were trudging across the parking lot.

He thought about the woman from the restaurant, the one who'd watched the latest chapter in his life unfold, and wondered what kind of life she had. She didn't seem the kind who needed a hand up. No, she'd been driving a huge truck. And her build had been strong, sturdy—not frail and wispy like Matilda or Susan.

She was probably heading to some nice, comfortable home, where family waited and the biggest conflict was whether the television was turned to a do-it-yourself show or a Hallmark movie. Jesse could barely even picture what that sort of life would be like.

A dark blue truck pulled into the dirt lot by the park. This town was hopping with trucks—his little Chevy definitely said "tourist." Jesse started to stand, hoping it was Jacob, but then the two little boys, who'd been all the way to the street turned and ran to the pickup.

Sitting back down, Jesse watched as they

attacked the man, who looked a little old to be their father, grabbing him around the legs as he stepped down from his truck and yelling, "Howdy, Mr. Jacob!"

Jesse again stood.

The man wore jeans, a tucked-in, long-sleeve shirt and an old brown hat. He reached in his pocket and pulled out two pieces of what had to be candy as he asked, "How's your mother?"

"Sleeping. She told us to get out of the house cuz we kept waking her up."

Jacob said, "I'll see about having you come out to the ranch one day next week. You can do some riding and help out a bit."

"Yeah!"

The two boys ran off, possibly to tell their mother, possibly to keep Jacob from changing his mind.

Grabbing a folder from somewhere on the front seat, Jacob closed his truck's door and ambled over to where Jesse waited.

"Park's a mighty strange place for a meeting. The restaurant would have been nicer, cooler. We could have had tea." He stuck out his hand.

Jesse awkwardly took it. Handshaking wasn't something he'd done much of lately. "Yes, well, we'd already eaten and—"

Jacob looked at Timmy and then back at Jesse. "You never said anything about a kid."

"This is my son. When my mother picked me up this morning, she introduced me to him. Before then, I didn't know he existed, and..." Jesse's voice trailed off as he tried to think of the best way to phrase the rest of it.

"And?" Jacob prompted him. He wasn't exactly frowning. He had more of a here-we-go-again look on his face.

"When she dropped me off at the restaurant, she left Timmy."

One of Jacob's eyebrows raised. "For good?"

"Apparently."

"Are you saying that the single ranch hand I hired really isn't single?" Jacob started shaking his head. "The position's not meant for a family man."

Jesse swallowed, and thought back to the Bible verse: *Have I not commanded you? Be strong and courageous. Do not be terrified; do not be discouraged, for the Lord your God will be with you wherever you go.*

In a voice stronger than he felt, Jesse said, "Sir, it looks like I'm a family man for a while, but that won't keep me from doing exactly what you expect me to do. I'm a hard worker. Timmy doesn't take up much room, he's quiet, and we'd both appreciate a chance. I promise you there'll be no problems."

Jacob still shook his head and stood. "Your quarters would be a room, one room, in the sleeping quarters with the other two hands. That's no place for a kid."

"It's better than the car where we'll be sleeping tonight. It's better than a shelter in town amidst a bunch of strangers."

Jacob didn't even blink. "I wish I had better news for you, son, but taking on the two of you is more than I'm prepared to do. I had misgivings about taking on just you."

He started for his truck, interview over. Jesse tried to think of something that would change the man's mind. Minutes ago, Jacob had offered a day of play and work to two little boys with a sick mother. That was the kind of boss Jesse needed in his life right now.

And Timmy probably needed it even more.

"Sir."

Jacob didn't turn around.

"Sir, I'll work for free the first week. You need to provide only a place for us to sleep and food."

Jacob opened the truck's door.

Before he could climb in, Jesse said a word he hadn't said in a long time. Not when they'd sentenced him, not when he'd faced his first adversary while incarcerated and not when he prayed.

"Please."

Chapter Four

It took Eva almost two hours to cancel all the details tied in with the wedding reservations. Next she handled one complaint—it was clear that the guest wanted to be upgraded to a suite rather than a single room without paying the extra cost. Eva hated giving in to such blatant manipulation, but fighting the point wouldn't accomplish anything. The ranch was nearly empty; Eva sent Mitch, one of the summer wranglers, to help with the move.

"And change into your uniform top," she said. Mitch too often wore casual T-shirts, ones that advertised not the ranch but either beer or taverns. Today's flaunted a place called Rex's Bar and Grill.

"Yes, ma'am," he said, without any respect in his tone. This was his second summer, and she hoped it was his last. He had a habit of disappearing when they needed him. Worse, some of the guests coming back from a trail ride complained that he didn't talk and was cold and unwelcoming.

She couldn't write him up for not talking, but it didn't make him her favorite hand.

Leaving Patti behind the desk, Eva peeked out the big picture window. Her father's truck wasn't in the main lot. Maybe he was down at the corral with the new hire. A real horse person would rather meet the horses than the owner's daughter. Right?

"You might as well call your father. We're both curious. Let's see how things are going," Patti suggested. "It's been over two hours since you checked up on him."

Patti never thought twice about calling Eva's father to ask questions, get advice and report. Eva never did, preferring to convince him that she could handle any problem herself.

Eva studied the expanse of desert and mountain scenery. Her home, and she loved every inch. "I think I'll go down and check things out again. We have the vet scheduled for today."

Patti raised one eyebrow; Eva rarely went near the horses. "I'm impressed. Twice in one day. If the horses faint, let me know."

Eva stuck out her tongue before exiting the main house, grabbing a helmet from the ATV's rear cargo box and hopping on. As she drove the half mile to the barn, she started second-guessing herself. The earlier visit hadn't been bad. But would she be able to handle this second visit?

To distract herself from her fears, she focused her mind on her other problem—namely, the ranch's business problems. Her father wanted the place to be a ranch first, and a resort as a distant second. Eva wanted to convince him to turn those priorities around.

In truth, the lodging part of the Lost Dutchman was less of a headache than the ranch part, the guests' interactions with the horses. In the past five years, once a guest had tripped on the tennis court, resulting in a sprained ankle. On the other hand, they'd had a dozen broken bones and at least one lost tooth thanks to riders leaving the horses' saddles before the planned dismount.

They needed to shore up the side of their business that made money with no liability. She wished her dad realized that. But, that was her dad, tunnel-vision. She couldn't get through to him that they needed to modernize the Lost Dutchman. Their business would triple if he'd agree to put in a water slide and a lazy river, plus a separate pool just for adults—but no, for the past twenty years horseback riding had been the main draw, and he was convinced nothing else was needed. He'd only reluctantly conceded to include guided hikes, biking and tennis.

And this new hire, this project of Mike Hamm

and her father, would undoubtedly be a horse person; summers on a ranch did that to boys. He'd just be one more voice shouting her down when she said they should have more to offer that didn't include horses.

Her red shirt clung like wet glue to her back as she parked the ATV and walked to the barn. To the left, a wrangler hired just two months ago conducted an intermediate riding lesson. Without having to count, Eva knew that half a dozen children ages seven to nine were involved. They were the only age willing to ride horses in this heat. Their younger siblings were in the craft house. Their older siblings were probably either in the game room or at the pool.

They'd definitely all be in the pool if only her father listened to her.

By the time she entered the barn, she was too relieved to get out of the sun to mind being surrounded by horses. She spotted Harold, their foreman and head wrangler, in Palomino Pete's stall. Pete was a quarter horse that had been in the family for decades. Eva had first sat on Pete's back when she was six. She'd last sat on his back when she was eight—the last time she'd ridden at all.

A family of wild turkeys had managed to get in the arena while she was riding. Maybe Pete had never seen turkeys before. Maybe Eva had gotten excited and accidentally kicked him. Or maybe he'd just stumbled at the wrong time, while she was too distracted to hold on.

No matter the cause, the result was that Eva had flown from his back and landed on her head on a rock. Thirteen stitches and one minor concussion later, her father had said no to her getting on Pete's back again.

She'd wanted to, or so Harold said.

But Jacob Hubrecht expected people to listen when he gave orders. Especially then, when Eva's mother had been just six months dead and nothing felt like it should have at the Lost Dutchman.

Right now, nearing retirement, Pete never went on the trail rides. He was used only for the smallest of children who wanted a safe, brief ride. In all the years they'd had him, Eva was the only rider ever to fall off.

"Everything all right?" Eva asked, not venturing past the entrance to the stall. "You hear from Dad?"

"I expect your dad any minute, and Pete's got a slight crack on his left front hoof," Harold said. "Probably be okay by the time tourist season begins."

They needed tourist season to start tomorrow! Thanks to the economic downturn, the Lost Dutchman Ranch couldn't remember what feast was and too often felt the tightening belt of famine.

The Lost Dutchman would make it, though.

Everyone wanted to be a cowboy for a day, week, month. Eva, who'd majored in marketing, knew how to promote the ranch. If only she could get her father to listen to her ideas.

And stop hiring unsuitable people when they could hardly afford the staff they already had.

"I really don't like this change," Eva muttered.

Leaving Harold to his job, Eva went back to the ATV and returned to the main house. Maybe the new hire hadn't shown up, and all the paperwork, phone calls and arranging for a bed had been a wasted effort on her dad's part.

If only she could believe that.

She parked in front of the steps leading up to the two-story adobe building that had started life as a one-room cabin. Only one wall remained of that original structure. Her dad had installed a pane of glass over it, and added a plaque that shared the history of the structure.

Her dad's truck still was nowhere around.

The current Lost Dutchman ranch house was pretty much the same color as the desert surrounding it and boasted a combination of Santa Fe style and Old West relic decor. The front porch jutted out and had what looked like tree trunks holding it up. A replica of a Conestoga wagon was to the left of the porch; a modern playground was to the right.

Stepping from her quad, she noticed that the blue jungle gym needed a fresh coat of paint. One of the rocking chairs on the porch had a rattan backing that should have been replaced. Only the cacti did their job without complaint. They looked hot and dry.

Like Eva felt.

She stepped into the lobby and pulled her shirt away from her body. The sweat dripping down her back instantly chilled thanks to the air conditioning. Patti turned the thermostat down to seventy-two every time she was left alone. It didn't matter how many times Eva cautioned her about the electricity bill.

"You heard from Dad?" Eva asked, moving back behind the desk to check reservations. No change in the last thirty minutes.

"No. He's been gone longer than I expected." Usually Patti had a sixth sense about Eva's father.

"What do you think?"

"I think he went into town, looking like he was on a mission, and he'll be back soon." Patti didn't say anything Eva didn't already know. The difference was, Patti wasn't curious.

"I'm back." Her dad's rich baritone voice came from the doorway.

Eva looked up just as he stepped aside to let the new hire in.

"I thought we'd come here first," Dad said. "We can show the little one the playground and game room."

The little one had a name, and Eva knew it.

Timmy.

She didn't know the big one's name. She knew only that he came with more problems than their little ranch could afford.

"Don't touch," Jesse warned as Timmy finally showed an interest in something and headed toward a large glass pane that showcased a dirt wall. Before Jesse could stop the little boy, he'd touched the wall and then fingered a woven wall hanging.

"That's okay," Jacob said. "Glass cleans, and that wall hanging is so dusty, it makes me sneeze."

Jesse didn't miss Eva's glare.

Jacob was oblivious. "This is my daughter Eva. She'll get you started on the paperwork."

"That wall hanging is more than a hundred years old," Eva muttered.

While Jacob bent down next to Timmy and explained that the wall hanging had been handmade by his wife's grandmother, Jesse stared at the blonde from the restaurant.

He should have seen the resemblance.

She was her father's daughter, all right. Jacob was a good two inches over six feet; Eva was close to that, maybe just under six foot, equal in height with Jesse. Her blond hair was as full and rich as her father's, though Jacob's hair was light brown. And unlike Jacob, Eva had dark brown eyes. They reminded Jesse of a stone he'd kept in his pocket when he was about Timmy's age. He couldn't remember the name, but he'd loved it for the color and texture.

Eva looked at her father as if he'd lost his mind. Jesse half expected her to refuse to help him. Instead, she took a breath, looked to him as if she silently counted to ten, and brought out some documents. "I put this packet together last Friday. But I'll need to add a couple more. We didn't know you were coming with…"

"A son," Jesse filled in for her.

She nodded. "Dad, you're not going to put them in bunkhouse. I don't think Mitch and the other wrangler would appreciate it."

Jacob straightened, saying, "Do we have an empty cabin?"

"Noooo," Eva said, aghast.

"Yes." There was another woman in the room, one Jesse'd almost missed. She, too, was tall, but unlike the Hubrechts he'd already met, she had red hair. Right now she was giving Eva a bewildered stare. She'd been watching the exchange between the three with keen interest.

"The Baker wedding party canceled, Dad," Eva explained.

He whistled. "That will cost us a pretty penny. What happened?"

The redhead answered, "The bride reunited

with her ex-boyfriend when he came home from Afghanistan." To Jesse, she said, "I'm Patti de la Rosa, I help run the place."

Eva interjected, "I already put all the cabins up on the website as a special."

"We don't need a cabin." Jesse just wanted out of this room and this debate so he could be alone—or at least, as alone as he could be with a five-year-old. "The bunkhouse you told me about is fine."

Eva raised an eyebrow.

"He can use the guest apartment," Jacob decided.

"That's for family," Eva said.

"The family hasn't used it in a good long time. It's just sitting there, wasted space."

Eva looked aghast. "But what if Elise decides to come home and—"

"She won't."

Something in Jacob's tone made Jesse believe him. Whoever Elise was.

"A single room is fine," he insisted.

"No, Dad's right. You'll need a bathroom." For all her indignation and huffiness, there was something about her expression as she looked at Timmy. Jesse saw then something he'd missed earlier when dealing with her: a hint of compassion. Not for him, but for Timmy, whose yellow T-shirt was torn and threadbare, who had stick arms poking from the sleeves, and who sported the kind of grime that came not from one afternoon spent in the dirt, but many. The kid's ears were almost black.

The kid?

His kid.

"We'll appreciate anything you can do for us tonight," Jesse said.

Timmy wasn't paying attention. It was almost as if when Eva started talking, he stopped listening.

"Come on, then," Jacob said. "I'll take you to the guest apartment. It's not been cleaned or aired out in a while."

"I know how to clean and open windows." Jesse fell in step behind Jacob. Glancing back, he felt relieved to see Timmy coming along, too—although clearly "speed" wasn't a word in the boy's vocabulary.

"This is the Lost Dutchman Ranch," Jacob said, as if Jesse didn't know. "I purchased her more than thirty years ago. I was just off the rodeo circuit, settling down, thinking of starting a family. She started life as a one-room cabin. You saw one of the original walls in there. I left it and put it behind glass."

If this was the desert, Jesse thought, it was the oasis of deserts. There were plenty of green plants and cacti. Every few yards, there was a swing with a canopy. An empty tennis court was to his left, and what looked like a one-room schoolhouse was to his right.

"Man I bought her from had built two more rooms, but neither was up to code."

Jesse wasn't sure what that meant.

"I added electricity, running water and furniture. A few years later, when my wife got pregnant with Eva, she insisted on a bigger house. I built her this when she had my third daughter, Emily."

"Is your wife the redheaded woman back at the main house?"

"Patti?" Jacob's laugh sounded more like a bark. "Patti de la Rosa works for me. She helps Eva run the business side of things. She's been a blessing since my wife died. More than once her advice on how to raise my three daughters kept me from falling on my face."

"No sons?"

"No, but my daughters can do just about anything that sons could do. Eva's the only one who stuck around, though. She was just a little thing when I started expanding the main house. I've got pictures of her mixing mud mortar. She thought she was making pancakes, I'm pretty sure."

"You built the main house?"

"Designed it, built it, maintain it."

Before Jacob could say anything else, they arrived at the barn.

"I'll introduce you to Harold Mull. He's the head wrangler and foreman. When I'm not telling you what to do, he'll be telling you. The vet's here, too."

Timmy had been keeping up, but now that they'd reached the barn, he hesitated.

"Come on," Jesse urged him. "Nothing's going to hurt you."

"Ever seen a horse before?" Jacob asked.

Timmy shook his head.

"Well," said Jacob, "they're my favorite animal in the whole world. Next to dogs, of course."

Timmy nodded as if he agreed.

Next thing Jesse knew, Jacob had both of them in the barn, standing next to a stall, as the vet took care of a horse named Harry Potter.

"My youngest daughter named quite a few of the horses," Jacob explained. "She always had her head in a book. Consequently, we've got some very literary horses."

An hour later, after introducing Timmy and Jesse to more horses and to the two wranglers, Jacob led them to a set of stairs in the back of the barn. The top of the stairs had a storage alcove on one side and the apartment on the other.

"We call this the loft and don't lock the door. You can if you want. I'll need to find the key."

The front door opened to a living room with an ugly green couch, a mud-brown easy chair, a scratched coffee table and an old-fashioned television. Timmy, uninterested in the tour, immediately settled onto the couch. The kitchen was behind it.

A door to the right led to a bathroom and bedroom big enough for only a bed, no dresser.

After showing Jesse around, Jacob cleared his throat and said, "You can start in the morning. Four o'clock. Harold will tell you what to do. Meantime, dinner is from five to six here."

The door slammed behind him, and for the first time that day, Jesse had silence.

He didn't trust it.

"Well," Jesse said. "Let's go bring the car down and unload our belongings."

Timmy's belongings, really. Jesse had a duffel bag.

No answer.

Timmy was curled into a fetal position on the couch, sound asleep. Jesse headed for the door, put his hand on the doorknob and stopped. Could he leave? Could he leave a five-year-old alone? What if Timmy woke up and got scared? Worse, what if Timmy woke up and wandered downstairs and out the barn door?

Five minutes later, Jesse carried the boy, who maybe weighed thirty-five pounds, all the way back to the main house. Eva stepped out on the porch.

Unlike most women, she didn't holler, "Everything okay?"

Instead, just like at the restaurant, she watched him. Her expression indicated that she already knew what he was doing, plus all the things he didn't know, and why and exactly how it would turn out.

He sat Timmy in the backseat—right where he first met the boy—and drove to the barn, parking by a blue truck, which must be the trademark for the ranch. Then he gently eased Timmy from the car and carried him upstairs and to the couch. Before he went back downstairs to unload the car, he snagged a blanket from the bed and covered the boy.

His son.

It took only ten minutes to unload the car and put their belongings away. Timmy's clothes went in the bedroom closet, which actually had drawers. His games stayed in the living room under the coffee table. Then Jesse meticulously went through every crevice of the car. He found the owner's manual but no title or registration receipt. He found a jack but no spare tire. After circling the vehicle, he realized the spare tire was already on the front passenger side. The only paper in the glove box—aside from receipts and other trash—had been the birth certificate. There was no other information on Timmy.

He had no clue if his son had been to preschool, the doctor or church. He was starting from scratch, both as an ex-con and as a father. A slight breeze pushed against him as he entered the barn and headed for the stairs up to his apartment. Instead of hundreds of convicts, he smelled horse.

He wasn't sure which smelled worse.

Entering his apartment, all he could think of was that for the first time in more than five years, he had nothing to do, nowhere to be and no one to avoid. Instead, he had someone besides himself to take care of.

Walking to the window, he stared out at sweet freedom. It existed. He put his fingers on the glass, probably not bullet-proof, and then felt along the frame, finally getting his fingers just under the edge. It opened, and he breathed in the fresh air—hot, tinged with the scent of animals and roiling heat…and yes, something sweet.

Chapter Five

Currently, there were thirty-two people seated in the dining room of the Lost Dutchman Ranch. Most were already finished with their meals and just sitting around, talking. It was too hot to do anything else.

"We really need more than eighty guests," Eva fretted, setting her tray on the picnic table closest to the kitchen door. That was another marketing strategy. She wanted enough guests and enough conversation to hide the sounds of clanking plates and Cook complaining about how slowly the potatoes were boiling.

"We have room for more than eighty," Patti said. "We don't *need* eighty. Your father's not worried."

"Of course not. He's sitting with the couple renting our number five suite in the Rawhide section. The man used to rodeo like Dad."

"Friend of your dad's?" Patti asked.

"No, but he found our place because he did a Google search for Dad's name. Apparently he's putting together some sort of rodeo reunion, and Dad's name was on his list. When he read about the Lost Dutchman Ranch, he decided to combine work and play."

"They look rich enough. Wonder why they didn't reserve a cabin?"

"Maybe they're rich because they know how to be careful with their money."

That reminded her. She'd watched Jesse at the diner peel bills from a small, dwindling roll. He was a man who didn't have much money to be careful with.

"Actually," Eva said, "they chose Rawhide because of the name. Thought it sounded Western. They plan to come again next year and stay in Boomtown."

Eva's father had named the lodging areas at the Lost Dutchman. The five suites were in a section called Rawhide. The five cabins were in Boomtown. The single bedrooms—seventeen of them, motel style—were in Tenderfoot.

"They're perfect guests," Patti said. "They already know how to ride, they like to hike without a guide, and the only complaint they've made had to do with the temperature going above a hundred and five."

Eva glanced over at the people. Both were

dressed in jeans and long-sleeve shirts, compared with the rest of the room—most in cotton shirts and shorts.

Shaking her head, she went back for seconds. Meals were buffet-style, a help-yourself kind of meal, with only one server walking around and making sure all the guests had what they needed.

The dining room was in the back of the main house. Picnic tables held guests, visitors and employees. The atmosphere was meant to be fun and relaxed. They did not serve a four-star meal. Tonight's menu was barbecue pork, beans and potato chips. All homemade by Cook, an ex-rodeoer. His specialty was Mexican food, but actually there wasn't a food type he couldn't produce.

As Eva returned to her seat, she checked out the back of the dining room where a kids' area—complete with a television for watching movies or playing video games—hosted about a dozen children of various ages.

At least ten of today's customers were not guests of the ranch but townies and tourists.

Absent were Jesse Campbell and his son.

Eva knew this because she'd stared down the path to the barn at least a dozen times. The little boy had to be hungry. For that matter, so did Jesse.

"Hey," Patti said, "you only got a bun."

By the time Eva came back with actual meat

on her bun, Patti had left to close down the front desk, and her father had moved over to join her.

"They're usually four o'clock eaters," he explained, referring to the couple renting in Rawhide. "Now they want to go relax. Imagine having time to relax."

Eva knew what her father's day typically looked like; relaxation wasn't on his schedule.

"So, Dad, why isn't the new hire here?"

"He called and said the little one was sound asleep and they'd be taking it easy tonight."

Eva leaned in. "Dad, did you get the whole story from him? About how he came to have Timmy?"

"Jesse said his mother showed up at the prison to pick him up. She had the little boy in the backseat. He claims he didn't even know he had a son, and apparently Jesse's mother wanted nothing to do with her grandson."

"He's telling the truth. I was at the Miner's Lamp when they pulled into the parking lot. I overheard the introduction." Eva wasn't sure where she was going with this conversation. She felt bad for Jesse, of course, and all that he'd gone through so unexpectedly. But what she really wanted was to express to her father was that right now, they couldn't afford another hand, especially one that came with a second mouth to feed.

"Hard to imagine having a kid and not knowing he existed." Her dad frowned and looked around the dining room. In the back area, a mother had joined her two children, and together they worked on a puzzle. Near the restroom, a young mother rocked a baby. On the wall above the entrance hung a portrait of all the Hubrechts. Jacob, Naomi, Eva, Elise and Emily. Smiling. Happier days.

"Everyone deserves a second chance," Jacob said. "You need to be a little more understanding. Mike Hamm says that of all the men he's studied with this past year, Jesse is the most receptive. When Mike was working with him, talking about career choices, Jesse kept referring back to his two summers working with horses. Kid had a rough childhood and made some mistakes. Maybe being here will keep him from making more. He needs someone to take his side."

"Kid? How old is he?"

"A year younger than you."

"What kind of mistakes? Why was he in prison?"

"You don't need to worry about it. I will tell you he was more an accomplice than outright criminal, and there's no record of violence."

Eva could only shake her head. "He worries me, Dad."

"Everything worries you."

"That's not true," she protested.

"Think of this," her dad said, waving a potato chip at her. "Jesse offered to work for free, just have to room and board. Now, really, who should be worrying? You or him?"

"Him," she said, humbled.

Her father nodded. "He kinda made me think of how the apostles must have felt, entering towns with no provisions, no bread, no money, no extra shirt. I didn't want to watch Jesse shake the dust off his feet because I didn't try to welcome him."

"That's a stretch, Dad."

"Is it?"

To Eva's chagrin, she didn't have an answer. Playing it safe and selfish didn't seem much of an argument.

Probably because she'd been using it too long.

Jesse sat slumped in the easy chair, watching his son sleep, and wondering how his first day of freedom could have gone so wrong.

Of course, it could have been worse. He'd heard of guys who'd immediately spent all their gate money on cigarettes, then robbed somebody and wound up back in the system before nightfall their first day out. Most of his gate money had gone—first to the waitress, and finally to the girl working at the convenience store—before he'd even had time to count it. But at least he had a window to look out of that wasn't covered in bars.

He looked at Timmy, still sleeping, and muttered, "Thanks, Mom."

Immediately he felt guilty. One of the scriptures he'd held close to his heart was Psalm 27:10: "For my father and mother have forsaken me, but the Lord will take me in."

Mike Hamm had scolded Jesse for using the scripture to avoid forgiving his mother.

Unfortunately, forgiveness was still a black seed of contention festering in Jesse's heart. Maybe—just maybe—there'd been a few thoughts about it when he'd first spotted Susan today.

Before his mother had said, "Meet your son."

Jesse bowed his head and said a prayer. It didn't escape his notice that after he said amen and raised his head, the first thing he saw was Timmy.

Who was, indeed, the spitting image of Jesse.

Okay, if Mike Hamm wasn't the go-to person, God was.

Jesse fetched his duffel from the bedroom. Setting it on the kitchen table, he stared at the old brown material. Another gift from Mike.

He'd been doing a study in prison, following the path of Paul. Tonight, Jesse looked out the window at the fading sun and growing darkness and realized that tonight, Paul wouldn't do. Jesse needed someone else. Who would Mike suggest? Who had Mike referred to when it came to trials and tribulations?

After ten minutes of reading, Jesse realized that he had two things in common with Job. First, the trials and tribulations. Second, both their names started with J.

Other than that, there were only differences. Job had always been a good and righteous man; Jesse was starting on year two. Job apparently had a loving family; Jesse, not so much. Job knew when not to listen to his friends; Jesse had been easily swayed by his, and look where it had gotten him.

Unfortunately, Job's mother—except for a reference to Job's birth—wasn't mentioned. Job's wife, however, was—and not in a good way.

Jesse skipped to the last chapter and found what he needed: redemption. Things could change and did. Where you came from, where you were now, did not necessarily have to define where you were heading.

He closed the Bible, rested his head on the kitchen table and closed his eyes, exhausted and hungry.

Well, at least he wasn't covered with boils.

Tomorrow he'd need to really clean the apartment. The Hubrechts had been telling the truth about it being shut up for a while. It was musty and smelled a bit of old mop water and neglect.

He slept for maybe two minutes before he heard the knock. Shooting to his feet, he stood disoriented for a moment. Loud noise. Someone was supposed to tell him what to do.

For five years, he hadn't made decisions for himself.

After a few moments, he hurried to the door. It could be Jacob Hubrecht changing his mind. Or maybe it was Harold needing help already. The head wrangler had been too busy working with the horses to do more than nod his head in Jesse's direction when they were introduced.

Instead, he opened the door to find Eva holding two plates of food and a half gallon of milk.

"You didn't come for supper, and I know the apartment's not stocked with food."

"Timmy's been asleep for three hours. I didn't want to wake him."

"I saw you carrying him to your car." She came in, making herself at home, and put the milk in the refrigerator and the food in the microwave. "You think he might be sick?"

That had never occurred to Jesse.

"I wouldn't know the difference between warm and hot when it comes to feeling a boy's forehead."

Eva moved to the couch and went to her knees. She felt Timmy's forehead, gently, even brushing his bangs away from his eyes.

"I have two younger sisters. One I helped raise. He's fine." She moved the blanket a bit, pausing and giving him a half smile. "Except he's wet himself."

"I...I..." Jesse didn't know what to say. In a

million years it wouldn't have occurred to him to check for that.

"You need to wake him up, get him in the bath and clean the couch."

"I can do it. You don't need to stick around. But—thank you. We do appreciate the food."

She nodded. "There are towels in the bathroom. Out the door and to the left, there's a closet with cleaning supplies. Pat the couch with the towel, don't rub."

"Okay."

He walked her to the door, noting how straight she kept her shoulders, how careful she was to stay ahead of him, not to risk touching.

She was slightly scared.

Of him.

"If you're scared of me, why did you bring me food and even come inside?"

She'd reached the front door, but at his question she turned, looking at Timmy and then at him. He didn't like the expression on her face, a mixture of sympathy and pity.

"I knew you were here and that you hadn't eaten since lunch and not much then," she said. "If you're going to work for us, you'll need your strength. I'm doing my job. Next time, though, I won't deliver."

She left the door open, reminding him to check out the closet and get Timmy cleaned up.

A sleeping son was easier than a wet son.

Son.

"Okay, kid," Jesse said, nudging Timmy's shoulder. A moment later, he nudged a little harder. Maybe too hard, because Timmy shot up, then hit the ground, and crawled behind the couch, to the kitchen, and under the table. He made his first sound, keening.

Jesse was grateful he hadn't keened at the restaurant during the hour he'd stayed under the table.

"Hey," Jesse said. "I didn't mean to scare you." He moved to the kitchen table, squatted, and immediately rose and stepped back. The keening increased the closer Jesse moved toward his son. The more he backed away, the quieter the boy became.

"You need to take a bath," Jesse said helplessly. "You had an accident."

Timmy obviously didn't care.

After five minutes, Jesse didn't either.

With keening as background noise, Jesse cleaned the couch and then ate a dinner he couldn't really taste. It was still fairly early when Jesse went around the apartment and turned off the lights. Timmy had fallen asleep again, one hand holding on to a chair leg. His other hand covered his face as he sucked his thumb.

Exhaustion and fear followed Jesse to the bedroom. What a day. In the end, Jesse didn't know if Timmy was more afraid of him, or if he was more afraid of Timmy.

This wasn't how his first night out of prison was supposed to be. Jesse'd prayed for a clean bed, a full stomach and the promise of a job.

Well, the Lord had answered that prayer. It was the intangibles that Jesse had forgotten to pray for. Last night, his final night in prison, Jesse had gone to bed anticipating freedom and opportunities. Tonight, his first night of not hearing the sounds of cell doors slamming shut, he felt only the chains of responsibility.

Chapter Six

Tuesday, Eva hit the ground running. A family of twelve had signed up for an early morning ride. Her father usually handled the venture but she handled the paperwork. They'd go three miles out and stop by an old cabin, where he'd prepare breakfast, talk a little about the history of the place, and when they were all ready—meaning when the Arizona July weather got too hot to bear—they'd head back.

Next, Eva was in charge of making sure a honeymooning couple got set up for a mountain bike ride. This time of year, early morning was the best time for most activities. Her dad—truly a jack of all trades—had already made sure the bikes were prepped. Now Eva had to put together a snack pack complete with water. After finding the perfect helmets and gloves, two people rode off, big smiles on their faces.

Eva doubted the bikes had anything to do with the smiles. She wondered what it was like to be as happily in love as they were. She had little experience with the feeling herself. She'd been in love only once and had come to find out that he was more in love with the Lost Dutchman Ranch than he was with her.

Another couple was going on a nature stroll. She put together a backpack loaded with water, lip balm and sunscreen, and a disposable camera. She doubted the older couple would be gone long enough to use any of it, but she'd been wrong before. Sometimes the Sonoran Desert made people feel young again and wander for longer than they'd planned. If they were lucky, they'd make it to a hidden waterfall or at least see some unique wildlife.

Once everything was set out, ready for pickup, she went into the kitchen and asked, "Where can I help?"

"You can start dicing the potatoes for hash browns," Cook said. "We have twelve guests signed up for breakfast."

Slightly stooped, more than chubby, and with dark tufts of hair on either side of his head and a swath of baldness across the top, Cook's real name was David Cook. Thus, he liked being called Cook. He was a great buddy of her father's and had traveled the rodeo circuit with him back in the day. His nickname had been Tumble.

Cook had first brought Jacob Hubrecht to Apache Creek. When Jacob stayed, Cook took advantage of the opportunity to join him.

"Combine that with the employees," Eva said, "and we're making breakfast for almost thirty."

She was never happier than when everything was in place. Today, though, not everything was in its right place. Jesse Campbell, still wearing clothes that were too big for him, walked in the side dining room door, looked around, and finally sat Timmy down at the table next to the kitchen door. Timmy, who'd obviously not taken a bath, didn't look happy.

"Not my business," Eva whispered to herself. "But, ew."

"Huh?" said Cook.

"Just thinking about the day."

"Never trust a woman who talks to herself," Cook said for the millionth time.

At sixty-five, Cook was still single.

Patti came through the door connecting the lobby to the dining room and hurried to Eva. She whispered, "They didn't have a good night. Something scared the little boy. The dad didn't get much sleep. He needs someone to get him on track today."

"And," Eva said, "my dad's busy."

"Yup."

Eva nodded, gathered up her cutting board and

potatoes because she could dice out there, and headed for their table. First thing she did was pick up the soda Timmy'd just helped himself to and say, "I'll pour you a glass of milk."

Timmy started to scrunch up his face, but Eva paid no attention. She dumped the soda and had the milk in front of him so fast he didn't have time to stop her.

"So," Eva said, conversationally, sitting at their table, "did Dad already fill you in on today's duties?"

"I watched as he brought the horses in this morning. I'm to follow Mitch on a ride at ten. Help with intermediate lessons at one. Then, start caring for the horses and equipment at three. I might help in the kitchen tonight."

That was new.

"You know how to cook?"

Jesse didn't bother to answer verbally; instead, he stood, walked into the kitchen and had a brief, muted conversation with Cook. He came back with a cutting board and knife exactly like hers. Next thing she knew, he'd taken half the potatoes. "I worked in the kitchen at prison. I can crack eggs, cook bacon, stir grits, too. Chopping potatoes is the easiest task of all."

And the one Eva usually was assigned. She wasn't known around the camp for her cooking skills.

Jesse quickly cut a flat side to the potato, set it

on the cutting board, and made perfect quarter-inch squares in half the time it normally took Eva.

"Probably a bit different here because you're cooking for a small crowd. In prison, I helped prepare more than a thousand meals a day." Watching his fingers fly and the beautifully uniform finished product, Eva believed him. If she tried to go that fast, she'd cut off a finger.

"Wow," Eva said, "you can cook and ride." The words came out a bit more sarcastic than she meant. It was a sore point. The one thing Eva Campbell wanted to be known for around the ranch was her riding ability. The Lost Dutchman was a dude ranch. Almost all guests came here with horses on their agendas. They asked her questions, wanted advice and always came back from a ride as if they'd had the best time of their life.

Eva hadn't been on a horse in almost twenty years.

Fear, white-hot and paralyzing, gripped her by the throat if she so much as put her foot in the stirrup. She put the knife down, dicing potatoes no longer a priority.

She hated that fear had a hold on her.

"I cook better than I ride," Jesse said and reached for the potatoes she'd not gotten around to cutting.

Timmy started to reach for a piece of raw potato. Jesse didn't stop dicing. "Timmy, I'm cutting these so they can be cooked. We'll have a hot breakfast a little later. Go wash your hands."

For a moment, Eva didn't think Timmy would move. But slowly, as if every muscle was sore, he stood and headed for the bathroom.

"He didn't take a bath last night, and he's still in the same clothes," Eva observed, not mentioning that the boy badly needed to change out of the soiled clothing. She was sure her facial expression portrayed more than words could.

Now Jesse put down the knife. "I woke him up, intending to have him take a bath, and guess I startled him. He started screaming. He crawled under the kitchen table and stuck his finger in his mouth. I wasn't about to crawl under there and drag him out. You were at the restaurant yesterday and heard everything, right?"

Eva looked down at the table, at the diced potatoes and knife, feeling slightly embarrassed. "It was hard not to."

"Well, I don't know what his life has been like for the last five years. I'm not about to scare him more."

He was right; she knew it. But if there'd been guests in the dining hall, it would have been an issue. Unkempt was one thing. Unkempt and smelly was another. Eva decided to change the subject to Jesse. "I'll give you a couple of Lost

Dutchman shirts. We supply them. Are those the only pants you have?"

Jesse's eyes flashed, just for a moment. Then he calmly picked up his knife and started on the potatoes again. "These are the only clothes I have."

"Are they the clothes you were wearing the day you were incarcerated? Did you lose weight?"

"No, these are the clothes Mike Hamm got for me. He misjudged a bit."

Her questions and offerings probably disturbed him, she realized, but she had a right to interfere. If he worked for the Lost Dutchman, he represented the Lost Dutchman. He needed to dress the part, or the guests wouldn't feel comfortable around him.

"You're not the first wrangler Dad's brought here hoping for a second chance. The first few weeks are the hardest. It's okay to accept help."

He looked surprised at that. "So, I'm not the first ex-con you've met?"

"No. But you're the first who also came with a little boy with special needs."

That seemed to surprise him, too. Maybe it was the way she'd phrased it—perhaps he hadn't realized that Timmy also needed help, just like him. They both needed to learn how to live normal lives. She had a feeling normality wasn't something either of them had experience with before.

He began the last potato. "Well, since you know

all about me, I might as well 'fess up. I don't have the clothes I was arrested in because they took them for evidence, and I never got them back."

He gathered all the potatoes into a pile, lifted the cutting board and carried everything into the kitchen. Eva kept eating, watching both the kitchen door and the bathroom door. Neither opened. She could tell by the noise that one of the delivery trucks had arrived for Cook. No doubt Jesse was helping to unload.

She hadn't a clue what was keeping the little boy so long.

When Jesse finished in the kitchen, he came out, looked at the table where Timmy should be, and stared at the restroom door, his expression half bewilderment, half concern.

Eva thought about jumping in, heading for the restroom and saying Timmy's name, helping out. She'd done just that with Emily, who at four years old retreated into her own world after their mother died. But really, this situation was so far out of her comfort zone that she didn't know how to climb the wall that stood between Jesse and her: prison record, troubled son, no ties.

Jesse Campbell was probably the most troubled soul she'd ever met.

And what exactly had he done that his clothes were considered evidence?

* * *

"Tomorrow you can come with me to run in the horses instead of watching. Then we'll catch the ones we need for the day." Jacob didn't so much as smile as he led Jesse from one horse to another. Some he stopped to talk to, stroke. Others he merely nodded at.

Jacob Hubrecht obviously treated horses like he did people. Some were up close and personal; others had to prove themselves. The wide-brimmed black hat he wore, covering steel-gray hair, was sweat stained. He had a red bandana around his neck and a pair of black gloves stuck in his back pocket. He knew his job and did it without hesitating.

Jesse followed behind him, Timmy in tow. Eva hadn't offered him a hat. The jeans she'd fetched from a closet marked Lost and Found were a little big, but not as big as the ones Mike's church had purchased for him. The button-down shirt with Lost Dutchman stitched above the pocket had creases and smelled new. Maybe that was a good thing. Perhaps it would keep Jacob from noticing Timmy's smell.

"Then," Jacob continued, "we'll cull the ones we need for the day, brush 'em and saddle 'em up. I'll guide you through the first few to see how much you remember."

"It's been a while," Jesse admitted. "I appreciate the help."

"Good attitude. Most of the horses weigh between eight hundred and a thousand pounds. I don't want you doing anything you're not one hundred percent sure of. You got a question, you ask somebody. If it has to do with the inside, ask Eva. Not much she doesn't know. Out here, you ask either me or Harold. We have two summer wranglers, but they know about as much as you do. We take turns saddling and going on rides. Part of your job is keeping our guests both happy and safe. You'll need to build trust with our guests, especially when it comes to their children." Jacob stopped in front of a pretty brown mare.

"This is Snow White. Now, before you make a smart-aleck remark, this here's my youngest daughter's registered Arabian/quarter horse cross. Yup, Emily named her, too, and as she's my baby, she can name the horses anything she wants."

"I haven't met her. Does she live here, too?"

"You'll meet her as she comes back from her summer studies. She's off attending college at the University of Arizona, majoring in Native American studies. Not sure how she plans on making a living with a degree like that. But my late wife was full-blooded Hopi. Emily's right proud of that. Snow White's almost fifteen years old. Emily was four when we got her."

There was a certain sadness in Jacob's eyes, but Jesse had no clue why.

"We use her for our guests who know how to ride and care about their mount. She's well trained but sensitive, just like my youngest."

They went past a few more horses, clearly Jacob's favorites, and stopped before a bay. Timmy, who hadn't been a bit bothered by Snow White, stepped back.

"This is Pistol. She's my middle daughter's. Elise is a barr...Elise *was* a barrel racer and roper. Basically Harold and I exercise Pistol. She's pretty lively, what we call high impulsion. Under no circumstance let anyone else ride her."

"And Elise comes to ride her?"

"It's been a long time since Elise rode her." Jacob's tone was gruff, and Jesse got the idea that something wasn't quite right between him and his daughter. He'd gotten that same feeling last night, too, when Eva had said something about Elise and the apartment. Then and now, he decided his best option was to keep his mouth shut.

"Are there any other horses that won't be used for guests?"

"Mine's Thunderbolt. He's one of the best quarter horses I've had. If I were younger, we'd be winning us some buckles. Right now, we use him mostly for stud. I can handle him, and so can Harold and Elise. I don't want you on him."

"Yes, sir." Jesse wasn't looking to volunteer.

"Harold's on his horse. He's the only one who rides that one."

"What about Eva? Where's her horse?"

"Eva doesn't ride. She's been afraid of horses since she was little. You might catch her down here a few times a week staring at Palomino Pete and thinking about getting back on."

"Just thinking?"

"So far she hasn't worked up the courage. Other than horses, that girl's not afraid of anything. Most straightforward filly I've raised."

Before Jesse could ask any more questions, Jacob moved on to a black-and-white paint pony.

Jacob addressed Timmy for the first time. "This is Pinocchio, even though she's a mare. Emily thought the name was perfect."

Pinocchio had compact body with one huge black circle on the flank and a black head. Her tail was half black, half white.

Going down on one knee in front of the horse, Jacob rubbed his hand along her neck. "It's been a long time since we've had a permanent some-one just the right size for Pinocchio. She won't run away with you. She follows whatever horse is in front of her. You think you can handle her?"

Jesse expected Timmy to run and find some-thing to hide under. Instead, Timmy nodded.

"Just one thing," Jacob said. "Pinocchio's got a sensitive nose. She likes the smell of children, but you know, she prefers clean children. You run back to the dining room, find Eva. She'll clean you up. Then, come back and you can go on the trail ride with your dad."

Timmy still moved like every bone in his body hurt. He looked back half a dozen times as if making sure Jesse wouldn't leave. "You'll be able to see me," Jesse called. "I'm staying right here."

Jacob whipped out his cell phone and called Eva. Judging from the one-sided conversation, Jesse got the idea Eva was less than thrilled about her task.

"When he gets back, he can come on the ride with us," Jacob said.

Almost immediately, Jesse realized that Jacob wasn't offering. He was ordering, just like he'd ordered Eva to clean up Timmy.

"I needed to talk to you about that, sir."

"I thought we agreed that you'd call me Jacob."

"Jacob," Jesse amended. "One of the things Mike Hamm drove home was the need to be honest, no matter the risk. I'm trusting in his advice and in God. I called my probation officer yesterday when I realized I was in charge of Timmy. I told the officer about Timmy and how I came to have him. He added me onto his schedule for today, but I need to be in Phoenix, with Timmy, at three."

Jacob's only response was, "Good thing I sent him up to Eva for clean-up."

"Not sure what she can do. There are lots of

tables to hide under in that dining room." Jesse filled Jacob in on last night's theatrics.

"You've got your work cut out for you. I knew you'd have to meet with your probation officer and soon, so no problem there. The schedule you have today is pretty much your set schedule. I'll expect you to work around it as much as you can."

Jesse didn't want to know what would happen if he couldn't. Watching Timmy sleep under the table had made one thing perfectly clear. Right now, the boy didn't need to be bounced around in uncertain circumstances.

For the next twenty minutes, Jesse helped with the horses, getting little tidbits from Jacob like "this one's bossy" or "he's a loner" or "I think she's got focus issues."

Jesse paid attention. Since serving time, he'd become an expert on paying attention.

Finally Jacob said, "Go on up to the ranch. See if Eva got the boy clean. The horses are ready, and the guests will start arriving in about ten minutes. It's hot, so we've only three going for a ride. They won't last long. And, for this ride, you're just a participant."

Heading up the path, he passed the blue two-door Chevy Cavalier. Today, he got a good look at the vehicle. The tires were bald, the left front fender was bashed in, and the paint was both faded and scratched.

Still, it was more than most convicts had the day after parole. He had a surprise kid and a surprise car. Neither were in good shape.

Jesse didn't feel top-of-the-line himself.

Two days ago, he'd been in a controlled environment: self-help groups, kitchen duty, shop work, getting locked in his cell. Yesterday things had definitely gotten out of control: released, picked up by his mother, finding out he was a father. What new surprises would today bring?

He walked past the dirt and cacti, passing two old Conestoga wagon replicas. Opening the front door, he noted the difference between outside—one hundred three degrees—and inside—probably low seventies. The same older woman as yesterday waved him through the door to the dining room and said, "I think they're out back. Took her a few minutes and a few cookies to get him out from under a table."

His footsteps echoed through the empty room. Laughter, the same he'd heard earlier but now closer, came from outside. Opening the door, he stepped on a porch and stopped, heart in his throat, unsure who he was most impressed by.

His son, Timmy, for actually knowing how to laugh.

Or Eva, holding a garden hose in her hand and dancing around while continually squirting a dripping-wet Timmy.

Chapter Seven

Thirty minutes later, Jesse and Timmy were on their first trail ride. A family of three were their guests. Both parents were terrified. Jacob had to bring out a stool for the mother to step on in order to mount.

Something else Jesse noticed was how Jacob made their ride personal. He knew the man was a Realtor in Salt Lake City. He knew the mom home-schooled. He got them to open up, talking about their jobs, so that they relaxed and stopped spooking the horses with their tension.

Their eight-year-old, Jesse observed, was a natural. Jacob started the ride by holding the reins and guiding the kid. Halfway through, he started teaching the kid: hold the reins loose; don't let him put his head down; he'll find something to eat and you'll never get him moving again. The kid was also amazed that Timmy, all cleaned up and also wearing clothes from the Lost and Found, didn't want to chatter or to shout "giddyup" or to take off as fast as fast could take them.

Timmy, showing forethought, moved Pinocchio behind Jesse's horse—the one with focus issues. Jesse had both their reins.

The hour ride ended in twenty-five minutes as the father never stopped being terrified. The mother did better, although she never let go of the saddle horn. All she could talk about was how hot it was. Heading back, Jacob talked the couple into investigating the pool while he gave Timmy and the eight-year-old a private lesson. Smart move, as the frightened dad didn't lose face in front of his son.

Jesse sat on the fence and watched as Jacob got both boys to mount and dismount multiple times. Timmy's head constantly pivoted as he carefully obeyed Jacob but also made sure Jesse didn't disappear. Next, Jacob had both boys practice how to halt and rein back. In the end, both boys not only walked but also trotted their mounts. Then, both boys helped with proper care as they unsaddled and brushed down their horses.

The eight-year-old ran to find his parents. Timmy came to stand by Jesse.

"He smells like sweat and horse," Jacob said. "Clean him up again and you'll have enough time to make it to town."

The apartment didn't look much different from yesterday. It was sparse and sterile. But it was clean. The furniture was ugly but it was all solid—nothing was falling apart. The roof over their heads was sound, and there were no dangerous neighbors. All of that combined to make it one of the best places he'd ever lived in.

"Do you have a favorite shirt?" Jesse asked.

Timmy didn't answer, just sat on the couch and stared straight ahead.

"Are you okay?"

Timmy nodded.

It was a response.

Jesse went into the bedroom closet and dumped out the garbage bags that contained Timmy's belongings. Last night, he'd looked for pajamas and found kid's shampoo, toothpaste, toothbrush and a handheld video game with dead batteries and no charger. The garbage bags, he soon discovered, had belongings that were not all Timmy's. Down in the bottom, he found some things that must have belonged to Matilda. They were tiny shorts and girly cotton shirts, all in pastels.

He couldn't imagine Eva in these. She was all elegance and control. These clothes were skimpy and ragtag.

He closed his eyes, trying to remember Matilda Scott. Truthfully, he remembered her apartment more. As for her, he knew there was curly red hair that went past her shoulders. She'd talked of going to college and Paris but she lived in front of the television, and her favorite place was a neighborhood bar. He'd never seen her in anything but shorts and short-sleeve shirts. She'd even worn them to job interviews. He'd always wondered if that was why she was always unemployed.

Truth was, she didn't feel real to him, almost like a memory he could question the validity of.

Except for Timmy.

The boys' clothes from the bag were clearly too big for Timmy. One pair of shorts had a sticky label on it reading 25¢. A tiny part of him hoped his mother had made the purchase, done something for her grandson. He peeled the sticker off, grabbed a T-shirt with a dinosaur on it, and headed for the living room.

This time, Timmy didn't crawl under the table. He shook his head.

"The ones you're wearing are dirty," Jesse argued.

Timmy apparently didn't care. Jesse tried a few more times, then changed tactics. "Go brush your teeth. You didn't last night."

Timmy refused to change his clothes, but he willingly followed Jesse into the bathroom—all without uttering a word.

"Okay, kid," Jesse said, deciding to give up the fight to get Timmy into fresh clothes. At least Eva had gotten him changed earlier. He'd rather introduce his parole officer to a kid that smelled like horse than a kid who smelled like urine.

Jesse pretty much did the same thing as Timmy, washing his hands and face, brushing his teeth. Once they were both spiffed up, he herded Timmy to the main house, snagged them both box lunches and headed for the Cavalier.

Which didn't start.

Not even one click when Jesse turned the key in the ignition.

What Jesse knew about cars could be written on a three-by-five notecard. He'd never owned one. He'd driven, oh yeah. The first time he'd driven, it had been at age thirteen when the phone in their apartment rang and a bartender said, "This Susan Campbell's house? She's passed out. Come get her."

Jesse had walked to the bar, all of four blocks away, taken his mother and her car keys, and driven home. He'd managed to ding two or three parked cars that night, and for the next few months every time someone knocked on the door, he expected the police coming to arrest him.

After that, he'd had a friend teach him how to drive.

Jesse spent ten minutes trying the ignition key again and again, raising the hood and staring at machinery he didn't recognize, and even kicking one of the tires.

It looked like it needed air.

"If you hurry," Jacob called from the barn, "you can catch Eva as she drives into town."

It was the last thing he wanted to do. She'd fed him last night, given him clothes, bathed Timmy and now it looked like she'd take him to his first parole officer meeting.

So far, all his first impressions sucked.

Luckily, she hadn't left yet, and when he told her why he was in a hurry, she'd set down the papers she'd been sorting and grabbed her purse.

"I really appreciate it," Jesse said.

"I was going to town anyway. Let's hurry and get Jesse's car seat."

"Car seat?"

"You do know because of his age and weight he belongs buckled in the backseat in a car seat, right?"

Jesse could only shake his head. Something else to learn.

Eva easily filled him in on the rules, which, of course, Jesse had already majorly broken. It was a relief when she finally found a car seat in the lost and found and then herded them all to her truck. She recited the address he'd given her to her phone. After a moment, a monotone female voice said, "Take Main Street, two miles, to H Avenue."

Even Timmy looked interested.

Eva ignored the device, started driving, and said, "It will take me about an hour to pick up what we need from the box store. Wait out front and I'll pick you up when I'm through."

The phone reminded her to turn at H Avenue.

"You sure you don't want me to wait?" she asked, suddenly looking unsure.

Jesse'd rather have a root canal. He'd been to places like this with his mother. He remembered seeing people down on their luck, people who no longer cared, and worse, people who had never cared.

This was not the place for Eva. Timmy either, but Timmy was his and had to see how things really were.

While Jesse and Timmy opened their box lunches, Eva turned on the radio, country music again. He remembered it echoing from her truck when she'd parked in the Miner's Lamp parking lot. Soon she was humming and even singing along to a few songs. Jesse recognized one as the song she'd been singing while spraying Timmy with the hose. Timmy must have remembered it, too, because his eyes closed, and he was nodding his head as if he enjoyed it.

Jesse wasn't much on country music. He'd always considered it depressing, and his life was depressing enough.

Like today. What would the parole officer do about Timmy? Could they take Timmy away? Jesse'd fight tooth and nail. The only way to make the kid stop hiding under tables was to give him a place that made him feel safe. And tossing him into the system would do nothing but make him more afraid.

Both Jesse and Timmy needed the Lost Dutchman Ranch. But before Jesse could perfect exactly what he was going to say to his new probation officer, Eva pulled into a parking lot in front of a two-story brown building. It looked old, well used and unassuming, like it wanted to blend in with its surroundings and not be noticed. Jesse understood the feeling.

He opened the door and hopped out, bringing Timmy as well as the remnants of their lunch with him. "Thanks."

"You're welcome. Good luck."

Jesse wasn't sure how much Eva knew about the ins and outs of supervised release. He'd need more than luck; he'd need compassion, guidance and understanding.

Most of all, he needed prayers, lots of them.

Timmy stared up at the building and climbed the front stairs slowly, his eyes glimmering. "Have you been here before?" Jesse asked.

Timmy looked around, studying the busy street,

the uneven sidewalk and the other businesses, before shaking his head.

"A place like this?" Jesse asked.

This time Timmy nodded.

"And what happened?" Jesse hoped for a response but wasn't surprised when none came. Instead, Timmy plopped down on the top step—facing the street rather than the building—wrapped his arms around his knees and started rocking.

Jesse'd been with the kid twenty-four hours and this was something new.

"I've never been here before," Jesse said.

No change.

Well, Mike preached about honesty. Jesse wasn't sure how it would work with a five-year-old, but he was willing to give it a shot.

Jesse walked a few steps to a trash can, praying to Jesus the whole way and trying to figure out what to say to a little boy who knew more about abandonment than he knew about Jesus.

Honesty was the only option.

"Your grandmother picked me up in front of the prison, remember?"

No nod, no acknowledgment.

"I have to meet the officer in charge of my case. He's going to read me the terms of my release, talk to me about what I can and can't do, and—" Jesse doubted the kid needed to hear about urine samples and such "—and then ideally we leave and find Eva waiting for us so we can go back home."

Home. The Lost Dutchman Ranch really wasn't home. It was a destination, and one he was grateful to have.

Timmy didn't move.

"Okay," Jesse said, "I'm thinking that you didn't come here with your grandmother, who turned you over to me."

Timmy gave the briefest shake of his head.

"Did you come here with your mom?"

Timmy shrugged.

"Well, kid, I've got to go in and do this now because Eva's not going to be happy if she has to wait for us. So, you coming in with me or not?" Jesse wasn't sure what he'd do if Timmy chose the "or not."

Timmy looked down the street. Eva's blue truck idled at a red light.

"I promise she'll be back for us," Jesse said.

It did the trick. Timmy stood and followed Jesse into a reception area. A moment later, Jesse was filling out information forms, and Timmy was drawing on the back of an advertisement.

Timmy was the only kid in the room.

"Jesse Campbell!" came a deep voice.

Jesse wasn't quite done filling out the forms, but he stood, knowing how to follow orders, and together he and Timmy walked into a small office.

"Trevor Winslow."

Jesse's parole officer had already returned to his desk. He glanced up from documents that looked like Jesse's release papers and said, "Tell me again about how you wound up with him."

Jesse retold the same story he'd shared yesterday on the phone.

"Let me see the birth certificate."

Jesse handed it over. "My name's not on it, but I think he's mine. He looks just like I did at that age. Plus, I did the math, and I was with Matilda nine months before he was born."

"Your parole doesn't say anything about restrictions, but since your name isn't on the birth certificate, we need to make sure you qualify as the boy's guardian. Kidnapping will draw you more time than assault and robbery."

Jesse looked at Timmy. "Your mom left you with my mother, right?"

Timmy nodded.

"Had you ever heard of me before?"

Timmy shook his head.

"First time you asked these questions?" Mr. Winslow asked.

"I wish I could say no, but yes, this is the first time. Yesterday, I was in shock and too busy trying to keep my job. Then, Timmy fell asleep last night before I could ask him any questions. When I tried to wake him, he had a bit of a meltdown.

Then, there's the issue that I haven't heard him talk at all. I don't think his throat or vocal chords are damaged, though. He can cry, keen and laugh." Jesse quickly described Timmy's behavior over the past day.

Mr. Winslow leaned forward. "Can you talk, Timmy?"

No response.

"Did you crawl under the table because you were upset, son?"

Silence.

Jesse waited, figuring it was best to let Mr. Winslow see for himself.

"He doesn't talk at all..." Mr. Winslow finally noted. Jesse wasn't sure if it was a question or statement.

"Not one word yet."

"We definitely want to step in and get him services."

Timmy started rocking.

Jesse, who knew enough to associate the word *services* with *removed from home*—and figured Timmy probably knew that as well—quickly said, "Timmy, this time 'services' means you meet with a counselor much like I'm meeting with a counselor right now. You'll meet with someone who will help you talk, if you can. Truthfully, though, you'll probably just sit in the office for an hour, and then the counselor will look at his watch, or her watch, and time will be over."

Timmy kept rocking.

"Just like you came with me today, I'll go with you. I'll even stay in the room if they let me," Jesse said.

To Jesse's amazement, Timmy stopped rocking.

"I don't wear a watch," Mr. Winslow said.

"Whatever we can do to—" Jesse looked at Timmy "—let him know he's safe. As for me, I have two witnesses who saw that Timmy was literally abandoned into my custody." After giving Mr. Winslow both Eva's and Jane's information, Jesse shared everything he could about Matilda.

Twenty minutes later, Mr. Winslow checked the time on his cell phone. They'd made calls to social services and scheduled an appointment with a child custody lawyer who did pro bono work and would instigate a search for Matilda. At the very least, Jesse needed her signature to assure custody. At the most, she'd face charges for child endangerment and neglect. *If* they could find her. Jesse wasn't holding his breath on that one.

They also went over the state's expectations of one Jesse Carter Campbell, which included keeping a job, attending an anger management class each week and having no association with known felons. All the do's and don'ts.

Opening the door to see Jesse and Timmy out,

Mr. Winslow also promised to visit the Lost Dutchman to see how Jesse was doing.

"Anytime," Jesse said.

"I'll be there soon. And you're sure this is what you want?" Mr. Winslow looked from Jesse to Timmy. "Usually when I meet with parolees, I'm worried that they can't take care of themselves. You're taking on a child, a troubled child, and you have practically nothing to offer him."

"He's mine," Jesse said. "And I'll do the best I can for him." Looking up, he met Mr. Winslow's gaze. "When I was his age, no one ever tried to do their best for me."

For the rest of the week, Eva saw Jesse only at breakfast and supper, which he now helped with. Timmy was a different matter. Every morning after breakfast, Timmy showed up in the backyard, waiting for her to hose him down.

Based on facial expressions and participation or lack thereof, she knew he preferred her country singing to her rock and didn't appreciate children's songs at all. He was no longer willing to wear the T-shirts and shorts he'd arrived in. Instead, he wore jeans, no matter how hot it was; a Lost Dutchman crew shirt, two sizes too big; and a black hat that looked a lot like her father's. So, she ordered one in his size.

Weekends were their busiest times. As it was

Friday, she figured today the best day to tackle Timmy's aversion to changing his clothes.

Must be a boy thing. Her sisters had both had aversions to keeping the same clothes on for more than three hours.

She had the hose ready when he showed up. She turned it on and sang the two songs he seemed to like best. He danced, laughed and kept track of where his father was. When she turned the hose off, she picked up a bag she had waiting on the back porch and showed him another pair of jeans and a clean Lost Dutchman button-down shirt. "I'm putting the ones you're wearing in the washing machine," she told him.

He looked at her, his face puckering, visibly shrinking.

"Don't give me that look," Eva said. "It's past time."

Her dad walked by and said, "Pinocchio doesn't like it when she smells better than you. Ponies are funny that way. Take the clothes, go in the bathroom, change and give Eva the old ones. She'll have them back to you by lunch."

Great, her dad meant for her to run and do laundry this minute just to make a five-year-old happy.

Timmy looked at Eva.

"I promise," she said.

Timmy still didn't look convinced.

"You'll be in them before lunch," her dad predicted. "Miss Eva will deliver them."

Three hours later, just before eleven, Eva finally sat down after making sure everything was stocked for the weekend. The craft room had pens, pencils, paint and glue; the game room had every video game in the right case; and the pool room was stocked with towels, sunblock and bottled water. Finally she could check the website and see if there were any new bookings.

She'd just sat down when Patti answered the phone. After a moment, Patti's eyebrows rose and she said, "Ohhhhhh" before passing the phone to Eva.

"Please tell me you haven't rebooked all the rooms," came a breathless voice Eva remembered. It was to Eva's credit that she didn't exclaim, "You're the runaway bride!"

"We've taken a few bookings. Brittney, is the wedding back on?"

"Yes, it's back on. I don't know what was wrong with me. I was such an idiot." For the next hour, Eva listened to Brittney's tale of regret and glory while rebooking rooms and again arranging for the wedding to take place at exactly ten o'clock at night because the bride wanted to say "I do" at the exact moment she'd met her intended.

Eva didn't ask for another down payment. Brittney was the type of person who revisited places that made her happy. Eva expected that every July 19, Brittney and her husband would be making reservations. Plus, the wedding would be next weekend. The odds of her canceling before the refund deadline were slim, meaning should the wedding be called off again, the rooms would still be paid for.

Eva finally hung up, pencil still in hand, ready to recalculate their reservations, when next to her, Patti was saying, "Ohhhhhh," again and handing the phone to Eva.

"This is Eva."

"Timmy won't leave the apartment. He's under the table and your dad said to call you." Jesse sounded vaguely peeved.

It was the first time he'd spoken to her in three days and she was more than annoyed by the jolt of awareness that had come at the sound of his voice.

"His clothes," Eva breathed. "I can't believe I forgot."

"He's wearing clothes," Jesse responded.

"He's wearing clothes I gave him this morning. I took his other clothes to wash, and promised I'd have them back to him in time for lunch. I put them in the washing machine and then got busy on the phone and forgot about them."

"Well?"

Now he sounded a lot like her dad, using just one word to convey a whole paragraph and then some.

"Give me thirty minutes."

Hurrying to the back of the house, she prayed that housekeeping had needed to do a load and switched her load from washer to dryer.

Her prayer was answered. It took only a moment to tug out the jeans and shirt. Next, she used the ATV to get to Jesse's apartment fast. Checking her watch, she smiled. She'd promised thirty minutes and had taken ten. See, she could keep promises.

Harold was in the barn, grooming Thunderbolt—her dad's horse. "Why isn't Dad doing that?" she asked, sidling from the entryway to the stairs leading to the second level. Her dad's horse was huge.

"He's giving a private lesson to a guest who wants to impress his kid," Harold said.

Heading up the stairs, she knocked, and when no one answered, sailed through the open door and went right to the table and squatted down.

"Hi, Timmy. I have everything here." She handed the folded clothes over. "I've told Cook to keep a plate warm for you. Where's your dad?"

Timmy just looked at her. She noticed how clean he was, how clear his eyes were and that he needed a haircut.

"I'll wait outside, by the quad. When you're ready, come down and I'll give you a ride to the cafeteria. That is, if you can be ready in five minutes. I have to make sure everything and everybody is doing what they should." Eva winked before adding, "Even you."

As she stood and turned, the door to the bedroom opened, and Jesse came out. He was dressed, except for his bare feet, but he was rubbing a towel over wet hair and his shirt was clinging in a way that made it clear his skin was damp.

He'd obviously just stepped from the shower and had no clue she was in the room.

She started to say "oops" but realized that although her mouth was open, no sound came out.

She'd thought him slim. Wrong. The clinging shirt made it impossible to ignore the solid muscles in his shoulders and chest. She lowered her eyes. Big mistake. Even his feet were interesting.

Interesting?

"Oh," he said. "I didn't realize you were out here. I was—"

"—in the shower," she practically croaked.

Behind her, Timmy started humming. It was enough to break the spell.

"I came to give Timmy his clothes. Remember, I told you I would—"

"—be thirty minutes."

She backed toward the door, feeling the blush take over her cheeks. "I told Timmy if he got ready to go quickly, I'd give him an ATV ride to the dining hall. I even brought a helmet his size."

Jesse looked away from Eva and squatted to

talk with Timmy under the table. "You want to do that?"

Timmy nodded.

"Good. I'll be down in a few minutes."

Eva hurried out the door, down the steps, and made her way to the ATV, for the first time not scared of or even noticing the horses at all.

Chapter Eight

"Here's your pay."

"I said I'd work for free for one week, just room and board." Jesse stood in Palomino Pete's stall. He'd just checked the horse's water and was about to provide dinner. Timmy played with an old toy truck in the straw just outside the gate.

"I paid everyone else," Jacob said, still holding out the white envelope. "And you did a good week's work. I figure there're a few things you and the boy need. Unless you change your ways, I'm happy to keep you on. I've not heard even one complaint. And I was worried I'd hear a few."

Jesse didn't miss how Jacob's eyes strayed to Timmy.

"Harold's impressed, too," Jacob added.

"Good to hear." Jesse'd not been able to figure out if the foreman liked him or not. Outside of a few orders—muck this, water that—Harold had said very little to him. The closest they'd come to a conversation was a pointed warning on Harold's part that Eva was a filly Jesse should leave alone.

The advice wasn't necessary. Jesse was smart enough to know the boss's daughter was look only, don't touch.

Harold Mull was an interesting man. He rarely spoke, but when he did, his words were direct and brief. He looked like he'd seen the world and then decided he didn't need to see it anymore. Horses were his haven. If you got in his way, you'd better be willing to work. If not, you'd better get out of the way.

Already, Jesse took pride that Harold was giving him more time than he was the other two wranglers. The one closest to Jesse's age, Mitch, needed lots of prayers. He had no direction. The other one had potential but definitely needed to stay away from Mitch's influence.

That must be why Harold kept assigning Jesse to work with him. Jesse'd never met anyone like Harold. For that matter, he'd never met anyone like Jacob Hubrecht.

Or his daughter Eva.

"This week you've been doing a bit of everything. We're happy with that. Tonight will be no different. We've got a crowd registered because it's the weekend. You might want to stick around the dining hall, see what goes down."

Jesse didn't miss how Jacob's eye perused him, like a prison guard, looking for weakness and attitude. Well, Jesse wasn't weak. He'd make sure he worked like no one else, do what he was told, hold on to this job.

As for attitude...he'd keep working on it.

"Harold and I sat down and figured out your semipermanent schedule." With that, Jacob handed over a paper. "Nothing's permanent. If we need you more in the kitchen, Harold will take on more. If Harold needs you, Eva and Patti will do more in the kitchen."

Palomino Pete nudged Jesse's arm. Absently, Jesse reached over with one hand and stroked the quarter horse's long neck. "I've been meaning to talk with you, Mr. Hubrecht. My parole officer is coming out early next week. It shouldn't affect my work. I'll still take care of—" Jesse glanced at the paper in his hand "—dispensing hay, grain and supplements to all the horses. The PO's name is Trevor Winslow. He wants to see firsthand that I'm gainfully employed and basically doing what I'm supposed to be doing. He'll have a few questions for you, but mostly he can follow me around as I check water buckets and clean stalls."

Jacob laughed. "City boy will enjoy that."

"Then I need to take off at eleven. I've got an appointment with a lawyer."

Jacob raised an eyebrow. "You got enough money for that?"

"Apparently this guy does some pro bono work. First consultation is free. If I have to pay for later visits, I'll think of something." Glancing down at the white envelope in his hand, Jesse said, "This will help. Right now, because my name's not on Timmy's birth certificate, I have no legal rights. To enroll Timmy in school, get him the help he needs, I've got to make sure the world knows he's legally mine."

"You sure don't take the easy way, son. But Mondays are our slow day. I'll talk with Harold. Any time you make an appointment, let Eva know. She keeps an online calendar that we all check. Wish we didn't need to take in guests. Then we wouldn't need no calendar. Used to be that trail rides, riding lessons and renting out the horses to California studios was enough."

With that, Jacob ambled out of the barn.

"Hear that?" Jesse asked Timmy. "We get to keep food in our tummies and pillows under our heads. God is good."

Timmy didn't respond.

However, the little boy willingly followed Jesse up the stairs to the apartment thirty minutes later. He washed his hands, like Jesse; combed his hair, like Jesse; and tucked in his Lost Dutchman shirt, like Jesse.

Together, both males walked to the dining hall. Jacob was correct. Friday night was the busiest day he'd seen so far. The smell of fried fish and coleslaw greeted Jesse as soon as he stepped in the dining room. The table where he usually sat cutting potatoes was taken. Toward the back of the room, Jacob sat with an older couple he'd been chatting up all week. The man, Jesse'd figured out from overheard conversations, was an ex-rodeoer like Jacob. Eva was at the door, leading a couple with three young children to a table. Two waitresses Jesse hadn't met were hustling orders.

For sure, Jesse didn't want to add to the work of others. A table for six held the two men he worked with. One was barely out of his teens, working here for summer wages and more interested in girls than horses. He talked big and said little of any consequence, but he had potential. The second was a bit older. Jesse got the idea that Mitch stretched the truth and wasn't vested in anything but Mitch. More than once he'd made a remark about Eva, nothing inappropriate, just flippant observances that it might be nice to win over the rancher's daughter who would someday own all this.

Mitch added something about then being able to take it easy.

Jesse'd kept his mouth shut.

Timmy wouldn't be welcome at their table.

Jacob waved him over. Jesse took the seat next to Jacob and put Timmy on his other side. A coloring book and crayons were already on the table. Timmy had just started coloring a horse when Eva came over, crouched next to her dad and whispered something in his ear. Jacob nodded, stood and headed across the room and out the back door.

"Trouble?" asked Jacob's friend.

"We've got a drunk out front insisting he's here to meet a friend," Eva explained. "However, he can't remember the friend's name. Harold's called the police, but until an officer gets here, the man needs to be detained. He shouldn't be driving. That's for sure."

One of the waitresses stopped and asked Jesse, "Fish, shrimp or both?"

"Both for me. Timmy, do you want both?" Jesse was getting good at asking questions that could be answered with a nod or a shake.

Timmy shook his head.

"Just fish?"

A nod.

"You like coleslaw?"

A shake.

"Fish and french fries for my son," Jesse said. He asked Eva, "Do you want me to go check and see if everything's all right?"

Before Eva could answer, a horn sounded and sounded and sounded. Timmy went under the table. Jesse said to him, "Stay here." When Jesse showed up at the dark brown Cadillac at the same time as Harold, two things were immediately apparent.

One, the man behind the wheel had passed out with his head activating the horn. Two, before passing out, the man had somehow managed to drive the car forward and run over Jacob's foot.

Which was still trapped under the tire.

Jacob's face was as white as the moon just starting to appear in the sky, his teeth were clenched and a watery sheen of sweat already dampened his brow.

"Daddy, are you going to faint?" Eva's voice came from right behind Jesse. Apparently she hadn't listened to his instructions to stay put.

Through gritted teeth, Jacob said, "I don't know whether I want you to back the car up or lift it off my foot."

"We ain't lifting it," Harold said firmly.

"Then back it up."

All Harold had to do was nod at Jesse. He opened the driver's side door—ignoring the scents of beer, cigarettes and sweat that greeted him—and started pushing the man aside. He was limp, thoroughly passed out. No problem. The best thing Jesse'd found in prison, after God, was muscles. Jesse had him on the passenger side in three seconds. Mitch and the other hand came out the back door. The younger one said, "Whoo."

Mitch didn't say anything. He scanned the scene before him, and his gaze finally landed on Jesse. Something shimmered in the man's eyes—anger, maybe resentment. Jesse wasn't sure. He didn't pay much attention to it as he backed up a good three inches.

"Yow!" was Jacob's only comment.

Too late to help with the rescue, one of Apache Creek's finest arrived. Statements were taken. Jesse, feeling more than uncomfortable, gave the cop his name, what he'd seen and what he'd done. He noticed the teen ranch hands stuck around. Mitch had disappeared. The Cadillac received a red sticker and was moved to a parking space down by the barn and next to Jesse's Chevy for later retrieval.

Eva took over. "Dad, we're going into town. Urgent care is still open for another forty-five minutes. We have enough time to get there if you don't argue."

"There was dirt clinging to the tire. It cushioned my foot. I'll be fine. I probably just broke a toe. Maybe two. I did it often enough during my rodeo days."

Jesse'd watched as Jacob hobbled from the Cadillac to the back porch. His face was still white, and his eyes were crinkled, showing pain.

"Don't argue with me," Eva said sternly. "Your rodeo days were before I was born. If you broke something, we're going to find out and do something."

"If something were broke, I'd know it and—"

"Be a shame," Eva continued, "if you had to go to this big rodeo reunion your friend is sponsoring, and you were limping just because you wouldn't get your foot checked out."

Jesse watched as Jacob reconsidered.

"Okay, but, Eva, you go back in and take care of our guests. Harold, you make sure the idiot doesn't have friends who show up later and mess with the horses. Jesse, you can take me to urgent care."

An hour and a half later, Jesse brought Jacob back to the Lost Dutchman. The man had a broken big toe. Nothing could be done for it, not even a tiny cast.

Jacob entered the house muttering about dumb luck and a fool waste of time. Jesse went looking for Timmy, who'd stayed behind with Eva. They weren't in the dining room. He walked all the way to the apartment—empty—and returned.

In the back of his mind, he knew he needn't worry. Eva would watch over his son exactly as she watched over her father and everyone else. Complaining about it a bit, but doing it wonderfully. He entered the lobby again. This time, instead of opening the door to the right where the dining hall was, he went to the left, following the faint sounds of country music and thinking he needed to get his own cell phone and make sure Eva's number was on it under speed dial.

He knocked, and after hearing a faint "come in," he wound up in the Hubrechts' living room, an area that he hadn't seen before. It was clearly a man's room. A couch was against one wall with two big leather recliners flanking it. An oversize coffee table was in front of the couch. The television was huge, taking up half of one wall; the other half belonged to a fireplace that probably didn't get much use. On the mantel were three wooden, obviously Native American, dolls. A grandfather clock as well as shelves of trophies and books occupied the third wall.

Eva took up the remaining space. She sat on her knees in front of a loom that looked to be made from tree branches. She was doing something with long strands of yarn. On the loom was a half complete blanket that resembled the one hanging in the lobby next to the original wall.

Jesse glanced around for Timmy.

"I told him to lie on the couch," Eva said, not looking up, "but when he started falling asleep, he got on the floor and pushed himself as close to the coffee table as he could go. It has a base, so he couldn't get all the way under."

She'd also covered him with a blanket.

"How's Dad?"

"He's got a broken big toe. They couldn't do much for it other than tell him to stay off it as much as he can. He's right behind me and can tell you more. I just wanted to make sure Timmy was all right."

"He's fine. I guarantee you'll tell me more about the doctor's visit than Dad will. He'll just say, 'It's nothing. Stop worrying.'"

"The doctor says it will hurt for about six weeks and that Jacob should think about wearing something other than cowboy boots because they'll be tough for him to get off and on."

"He's gonna love that," Eva said.

Jesse felt a half smile coming on; he hid it. Walking over to where she sat, he noted that the loom was made from poles, not branches. It looked old, but well cared for.

"Yours?"

"Passed down from my mother and her mother before that."

"What you're making looks like the blanket on display out front."

"That one my mother made. I sell mine, sometimes here to guests but otherwise at the museum in town."

"How much do they go for?"

"Depends on the design and the materials I use.

This one will go for between five hundred and six-fifty."

Jesse let out a low whistle. "How long does it take you to make one?"

"About four months, longer if the ranch is busy. I make baskets, shawls and mats, too. Those are quicker."

It didn't seem to matter if she was working on the computer or weaving. Eva's fingers flew. Near as he could tell, she had more than a hundred strands of white yarn draped down from the top of the loom. From the bottom up, horizontally, came the colored strands that formed the design. She pulled yarn in and out of the strands. Every once in a while, she used something that looked like a fork that pat, pat, patted the woven yarn tightly together. There was also a narrow piece of wood in the middle of the yarn that moved up and down and seemed to help tighten the creation.

Her face was more relaxed than he'd seen it. But then, every time he was around her, she was either rescuing him or annoyed with him. He liked watching this at-peace Eva.

"You're good," he said.

"Compared to what? You've never seen a woman weaving," she responded.

She had him there.

"And this is what you do in your spare time?"

"Every moment I can find."

In his world, his old world, the women he'd hung around used their spare time to party. None of them looked at peace. Something he hadn't felt in a long time rose up in him, a longing for the type of life he'd seen only on the Hallmark Channel.

Not his world.

To keep from staring at Eva, he walked over to the fireplace. "These dolls look old."

"Depends on your definition of old," Eva said. "Those are kachina dolls. The middle one is mine. My grandfather carved it, and I remember my mother using it to teach me things. If you look closely, you'll see some of my teeth marks. I guess I liked to chew on it."

He studied it for a moment, noting how the wooden head was about the same size as the waist, how its wooden arms were at its sides and bent slightly, how the ears stuck out. It wore a white-and-green carved skirt as well as a hat shaped somewhat like a cake.

Jesse didn't have one souvenir from his childhood, just a few photographs taken by parents at school, other kids' parents, and then handed over to him.

"The other two belong to my sisters. When they were born, my grandfather had passed away, so one of my uncles carved them."

"Are they worth a lot?"

"Priceless," Eva said.

He nodded, moved over to the bookshelves and read titles. He pulled an old leather volume out. Instead of words, he saw hieroglyphics.

"The books are all about Native American life. Some are quite old, like the one you have in your hands. Most belonged to my mother. They're my sister Emily's now."

"She's the one away at college, right? Your dad says she comes back every once in a while."

"She's a junior, done with the core classes and taking the classes she loves. Right now she's on a summer project up in South Dakota."

"What kind of project?"

"She's recording oral histories of the Hopi."

"You're half, right?"

"Dad has been talkative."

Jesse quickly put the book back and picked up a trophy.

"My sister Elise's. She was a barrel racer. She also ropes. She was a national high school rodeo finalist in breakaway roping. Dad wanted her to follow in his footsteps."

"Did she?"

"No, her footsteps went in another direction." Eva stopped weaving and settled cross-legged facing him. "She's someone you might want to talk to. She's a social worker over near Two Mules, Arizona."

"Never heard of it."

"It's small—smaller than Apache Creek. We've always had the allure of the real Lost Dutchman Mine bringing in tourists. Two Mules has no focal point. It's just a community of people trying to survive and, according to my sister, most of them are messing up."

"Messing up," he echoed. "Is that why I need to talk to her?"

Eva looked out the window, her cheeks coloring. "No, of course not. Elise deals with a lot of little kids who've had tough times. Dad had me put your Monday appointments on the calendar. You're doing the right thing trying to get custody, and you're going to all the just-out-of-prison meetings, but we need to get Timmy some help, too. School starts next month. We have to find out if he can talk."

Jesse noticed two things. One, Timmy might be asleep under the table, but for the first time, he wasn't sucking his thumb. Two, Eva had said "we."

We?

Saturday morning started with a bang. Two families showed up at just past seven, wanting their rooms, even though check-in was at eleven.

In July, there were rooms available.

The first family wanted to know what to do with their two children. Eva handed them a schedule.

"But," the mom said, "the first supervised event isn't until nine o'clock."

"Yes, our activities start after breakfast." For a moment, Eva was very much afraid the mother would say, "What do I do with them until nine o'clock?" But the dad took over and said, "Honey, we need to get situated in our room, and then we can head for breakfast. It's from when to when?"

"Seven to nine."

She personally walked the second family to their cabin. They were return guests and knew the way, but she wanted them to feel welcome. During her return trip, she saw Jesse and Timmy in one of the riding arenas, working with a boy about Timmy's age.

Private lessons were always good, both because the ranch made more money but also for the student because they learned more. But she wondered if the parents would be upset to know that the man teaching their children how to canter had been out of prison only five days. She hoped that on Monday, when Jesse's PO showed up, he'd blend in so no one knew exactly why he was here.

With that in mind, she headed for the living room and settled on the couch to phone her sister Elise. Saturday mornings were the best time to reach her. Friday, Elise was on call because that was always when one of her cases needed her.

Saturday, many of her cases would be sleeping off hangovers.

After Elise answered, Eva spilled everything she knew about Timmy, ending with "and he doesn't talk, not a word."

"Does he make any noise at all?"

"He can laugh and squeak. Jesse said he keens when he's upset or scared. What do you think? Is there a chance he knows how to talk or can learn?"

"I can't make a judgment call on what he can and cannot do until I meet him, but I think your Jesse is doing the right thing. Until he establishes custody, all records will be closed to him. Do you think Timmy is autistic?"

"Huh?"

"Does he shy away from social activities? Does he do the same thing over and over? Like find something to do and be unable to tear himself away?"

"I don't think so. Right now he follows Jesse around, and if there's not something he can do to help, he finds something to play with quietly."

Elise sighed. "Without being there, I can't really say."

Unspoken were the words "and I'm not about to visit."

"Look," Elise continued, "there are a dozen different domains of autism. But you say the little boy was literally dumped on a dad who didn't even know the kid existed. Plus, he was dumped by a grandmother who herself had the kid dumped on her. Then, there's a mother we know nothing about, except that she snuck out the window to ditch her child without even saying goodbye. It's obvious he's been through a lot. This could be selective mutism. The sooner he gets help, the better. Right now the best advice I can give is to make sure Jesse completely lays out Timmy's day every day. Have him tell the kid what they're doing in the morning, afternoon and evening. Then don't stray from the plan. That will build trust. Timmy will feel safer if he knows what to expect. Call me when Jesse has custody. I'll—" Elise paused "—I'll meet you half-way and give Jesse some other recommendations."

"Thanks. Timmy's a neat kid. You can just see it waiting there, buried."

"Most buried treasure is never recovered."

"You didn't used to be this jaded," Eva said.

After a moment, Elise responded, "I know. I took this job thinking I'd make a difference. I'm not. I think you've got more of a chance with Timmy than I do with the thirty-two people I have in my caseload."

Eva waited. Elise wasn't usually this negative. There had to be something more going on here.

Finally, Elise burst out with, "One of my teen-age girls overdosed last night. She'll live, but she's ruined her kidneys, and her hair is falling out in chunks. She has a three-year-old. I'm heading back to the hospital in an hour. I'm hoping there will be something good for them to tell me."

"Why don't we get together next week?" Eva suggested. "Just the two of us. Two sisters, no talking about problems. We'll just go shopping and—"

"Sounds like a good idea. I'll look at my calendar and get back to you."

When Eva hung up, she knew next week wouldn't happen. Elise's calendar was full, always.

For the next four hours, Eva lost herself in the hands-on business of running a ranch. After breakfast, she spent most of her time with wedding details, contacting all the vendors to reinstate the orders she'd canceled just last week. The Lost Dutchman hosted between ten and twenty weddings a year, usually in the winter. July weddings were few and far between. Finally she headed for the kitchen to talk to Cook about the meal before the wedding.

Because the bride and groom were getting married late evening—smart in the Arizona July heat—the meal was happening first.

"How much help do you need?" she asked.

Cook sat at a booth in the corner of his kitchen. Reaching in his pocket, he pulled out a notebook and said, "If you can spare Jesse for a whole day, then I'll need just one more."

"You're kidding."

"Nope, he's good."

"It's starting to worry me," Eva said, "how well he's fitting in after just five days." What was really worrying her was how well he was fitting in with her as someone she noticed too much and looking forward to noticing way too often.

"Yeah," Cook agreed. "I wonder how he'd be doing if he didn't have the boy. Motivation's a strong guide."

Eva could only look at Cook. He'd never been motivated by anything, not that she knew of. Still, Cook did what he was supposed to. He was laid-back, never hurried and was content to work for them when his talent could have led him to bigger things.

Eva went back into the dining room. They'd be putting extra tables in, rented already and paid for by the bride's family, who'd also be decorating the room after lunch come next Saturday, taking it from rustic cowboy to white flowers and silk. Eva just hoped they managed to take everything down before breakfast on Sunday.

Checking her watch, she realized it was about time for Timmy to show up for his daily spray-down. Funny how that activity had worked its way onto her calendar.

Stepping out on the back porch, she looked toward the corrals and decided to be brave. She'd ride the ATV down there and tell Jesse about her conversation with her sister. Then she'd offer Timmy a ride back to the main house on the quad. Truthfully, she'd been down to the stables more this past week than she had in the last six months.

Before she could change her mind, she hopped on the ATV and rode to the barn. Today she didn't feel her chest tightening or her throat closing right away. It came a moment later, when she heard a snort and then one of the horses pounded the ground with its hoof. She swallowed, willing courage to come to the surface.

At this time of day, there might be a few horses in their stalls. None, she knew, would lean toward her expecting a treat or recognizing her scent. She was of their world but not in it.

Jesse didn't seem bothered by the beast that currently towered over and outweighed him. He stood next to Thunderbird, her dad's horse, and talked to him. Her father was there, too, favoring one foot and grumbling about how to mount.

"I broke my toe twice in my twenties," her dad told Jesse. "Believe me, I'd rather be run over by a Cadillac than stepped on by a bull. But back then, a little thing like this didn't slow me down a bit. I just vaulted back on. In my thirties, I hopped back on. In my forties, I carefully maneuvered my way back on. I'm sixty-four right now, and I think I'll need to stand on a big step stool to get on my horse."

Eva moved farther into the room and made a suggestion. "Why don't you let someone else take the trail ride today?"

"Because," her father said, "if I don't get back on now, I might never get back on at all."

Suddenly Eva felt out of breath. The stalls started to close in one her, trapping her. She couldn't breathe, needed to escape. Now. Stepping back, she turned, seeing Jesse's concerned expression and her dad's stoic one—this wasn't the first time she'd had a panic attack in the barn—and made it two paces out the door.

A squad car slowly stopped in her path. Officer Sam Miller, a friend from high school and now a cop, got out.

"Afternoon, Eva," he said. "You have any idea how that stolen blue Cavalier got on your property?"

Chapter Nine

"It b-belongs to Jesse," she stuttered and immediately wanted the words back.

And she now knew the cure for anxiety attacks: just have a police cruiser appear in front of you.

"That drunk get out of jail yet?" Jacob asked Sam as he exited the barn. Jesse and Timmy followed.

"No, he's still there," Sam told her father. "When I left, he was trying to decide who to call. That's not why I'm here. As I was pulling out last night, I just happened to glance at the blue Cavalier parked next to the barn. Something about it bothered me all night. I remembered the first three numbers from the plate, so I ran it about an hour ago. Sure enough, it's been reported as a stolen car, taken from Glendale, Arizona, three weeks ago. Eva says it belongs to Jesse." Sam looked from Jacob to Jesse, lingering on Jesse purposefully. "I remember you from last night. You're new here. Do you have something you need to tell me?"

For a moment, Eva watched the changes in Jesse's expression. She had a fleeting glimpse of stark fear. Funny, she hadn't seen that expression on Jesse's face before—even when Timmy was dropped in his lap. Fear quickly evaporated, replaced with something Eva couldn't quite name. It was the same hard look her father got when he wanted people to listen to him, to obey. That look, too, disappeared—replaced by a fierce calmness.

"No, I don't have anything to tell you," Jesse said, his words low and decisive.

Eva wanted to scream. It was unfair. She knew he hadn't stolen the car. "Look, Sam, I—"

Jesse held up his hand, halting her words. "I'm Jesse Campbell. I'm working here. You say the car's stolen?"

"Reported three weeks ago."

"I was in Florence State Prison three weeks ago," Jesse admitted, his voice steady and firm. "So I couldn't have taken it."

Eva caught the surprised and dismayed look that passed between two of the ranch hands as well as a few of their guests who'd moseyed over to see what was going on.

"But," Sam continued, "you admit you're in possession of it now, in possession of stolen property."

"I had no idea it was stolen. I thought..." Jesse paused.

"Can we move this conversation somewhere private?" Eva jumped in. She needed to get Jesse away from the crowd, do a little damage control, help somehow. For Jesse's sake and for her own. She certainly didn't need the guests to come questioning her about employee backgrounds.

She well knew the stigma that followed an ex-con out of prison. The Lost Dutchman had employed more than its share, but never before had an ex-con's background been so blatantly announced; never before had Eva cared if one actually stayed.

For Timmy's sake, she'd do what she could.

Sam agreed. "Sure, we can take it down to the station."

Eva looked past Jesse at Timmy, who'd been playing with his truck in the dirt and now sat perfectly still, listening. Her father frowned, clearly not liking the fact that two times now, within twenty-four hours, cops had been on the premises, upsetting the guests.

"Sam," Eva said, "I'll vouch for Jesse. I know the whole story about the car. I was there when he got it."

Now the spectators were looking at her.

Officer Sam Miller seemed undecided.

"His mother turned it over to him, just left the keys on the restaurant table. Jane de la Rosa witnessed the exchange, too. Honest, there's no way he could have known the vehicle was stolen."

Instead of responding, Sam phoned his captain—and put a red sticker on the blue Cavalier.

"My fingerprints are all over that car," Jesse muttered.

"My dad must love the fact that our ranch is becoming a dumping ground for vehicles that need to be towed. The one from last night is still here," Eva muttered louder.

Her dad didn't disagree. He just nodded at Eva and said, "Get it straightened out. I trust you." To Jesse he said, "You take care of this mess. I'll watch the boy."

Jesse went over to Timmy and knelt down. "You know I didn't take the car, and you know that policemen do their jobs and are fair. I'll be back as soon as I answer all their questions. Miss Eva's going, too. She'll help."

Timmy took matters into his own hands. In two steps he was at Jesse's side, reaching for Jesse's fingers and holding on tight. Apparently he was coming along for the ride.

Sam ended his phone call and told Eva he'd see her and Jesse at the station before he got back into his cruiser. "I'm surprised you can ride with me," Eva said as Jesse and Timmy followed her to one of the ranch's trucks.

"Officer Miller has no proof I stole that vehicle, so he can't arrest me."

Eva heard the unspoken concern in Jesse's voice and knew he was mentally adding the word "yet."

She started the vehicle and headed down the drive. The squad car was right behind her. Jesse's fingers tap, tap, tapped against the passenger-side door. In the middle, Timmy picked up an old and wrinkled Lost Dutchman flyer and pretended to read it.

"Don't worry," Eva said as they bumped across the dirt road just down from the Lost Dutchman and onto pavement. "I know you didn't steal that car."

"You might be the only one who knows that."

"My dad knows it, Jane knows it, and most important Timmy knows it."

Timmy nodded.

Jesse's fingers stilled for a moment before forming a fist and then relaxing. Looking out the window, in a low voice he asked, "You know what the prison guard said as I stepped out of Florence State Prison?"

"What did he say?"

"He said, 'See you soon.' And you know, it's only been five days and already I'm heading to the local police station because somehow I'm mixed up in a crime."

"Totally out of your control," Eva reminded him.

"I've got to do better than this. I've got a son."

Eva tried to think of something else she could say, something to encourage this man she barely knew. Finally she said, "Mike Hamm knows you didn't steal that car."

"You know Mike?"

"I've known him just about all my life. When he was a teenager, he worked for us. Plus, you're not the first ex-con who's worked on the ranch. I've told you. We've had at least three that I can remember, all sent our way by Mike."

"Anybody who works there now?"

Eva hesitated. On the one hand, Jesse needed to know that ex-cons could be successful. On the other hand, she'd be betraying a confidence. Luckily, Jesse seemed to understand her hesitation and changed the subject.

"Inside prison walls, the main complaint is 'Can't get a fair break.' I wish I didn't still feel that way."

"You're not inside," Eva reminded him. "Out here, in God's country, we tend to say, 'With God, all things are possible.'"

"Yeah, right."

"So," Eva pressed, "if you had to guess, who do you think stole the car? Your mother or your ex-girlfriend?"

Jesse opened his mouth, closed it and didn't answer. At least he wasn't staring out the side window.

"I don't know," he finally admitted. "Could be either. But my mother said Matilda left it behind. Why would she lie?"

"Matilda stole it, then." Eva nodded. "It had to be her. If your mother knew the vehicle was stolen, surely she wouldn't have left you with the keys. Not when you'd just been released from prison."

"Because in your world, parents care about their children," Jesse said slowly. Then he added, "I wasn't raised in your world."

Eva didn't know how to respond. He was right, but this didn't mean he couldn't be part of that world now. "People change," Eva said. "What was Matilda like? Why do you think she didn't let you know about Timmy? Was she older than you?"

Jesse frowned. "What made you ask that?"

"It's an old name—hasn't been popular in years. Eva's an old name, too. People are always asking me if I'm named after my grandmother or something."

"I don't know how she got the name, but Matilda wasn't old. Maybe she was five years older than me. But she sure didn't act it."

"Was she the type to steal a car?"

Jesse seemed to take a moment to gather his thoughts. "Matilda didn't own a car when I lived with her. Our apartment consisted of cast-offs and innovation. I remember making a coffee table out of a door and some bricks. She found a dresser abandoned in an alley with two drawers missing, and we lugged it home. Our curtains were beach towels. I don't know. It's been five and a half years since I last saw her. She…"

Eva waited a few seconds, then said, "Come on, Jesse, you have to have some opinions. Would Matilda steal a car?"

"Well, I don't think it was my mother."

Conversation ended as Eva pulled into the parking lot of Apache Creek's small police station. She'd driven by it many times, but she'd never had cause to enter.

Jesse opened the car's door, helped Timmy out and started around to open hers, but she beat him to it. The July sun lit the way, reminding Eva of Monday, the day she'd met Jesse, just five days ago. Jesse managed to open the door to the police station before she could get to it, and he motioned her inside. Tension rolled off him in waves. He had his hands in his jeans pockets, and she got the idea they were shaking.

For one crazy moment, Eva wanted to reach out, take his hand in hers and hold on.

Jesse settled in one of the hard, ugly green chairs in a waiting room boasting outdated magazines and one lone bright orange ball cap, advertising Rex's Bar and Grill, left on an end table. Timmy settled in next to him, quiet.

Eva carefully perused the wanted posters on the bulletin board, and Jesse refrained from asking if she recognized anybody. He hated this. She looked a little in awe of the police station. He'd seen it happen before. Six months before he went to Florence, he'd palled around with a guy who'd gotten arrested. Jesse remembered the girlfriend coming to the station to pick them up.

She'd been in awe, too.

A few months later, she'd been arrested herself.

Watching Eva look at the awards and certificates, framed on the wall and earned by Apache Creek's finest, Jesse wanted no part in her presence here.

It was wrong.

Still, he forced himself to sit still as she explored a side room with a table up front and lots of chairs. She paused in front of the photographs of officers of the law as well as a memorial to the only law officer in Apache Creek to be killed in the line of duty.

"I don't remember him," Eva said.

"You want a tour?" Sam asked, coming through the front door.

"Yes," Eva said.

"No," Jesse said louder.

"I've never been in a police station," Eva told Jesse. "I may never get the chance again."

The tour only took a few minutes. Eva looked impressed when they finally returned to the lobby.

Officer Miller escorted them to a back office, handed both of them a form to fill out, settled Timmy in another ugly green chair just outside the door and left. Eva sat, clipboard in hand, and started filling in information.

She didn't hesitate at all. She had nothing to hide. This time the seats were brown, not hard plastic, but barely more comfortable. As Jesse sat, he continued to watch Eva, reading over her shoulder. He got her age, her birthday and a few more details before she stopped and asked, "Well, are you going to fill yours out?"

"There's not one question on here that they don't already know the answer to," Jesse said matter-of-factly.

She looked around the room. It was small, windowless, a sick gray color. Typical for a small-town police station—almost indistinguishable from the others Jesse had been in at one time or another. The only difference was, this time he wasn't guilty. All the other times, he was. He'd done the shoplifting, been out after curfew, been truant and consumed alcohol while underage. Luckily, those transgressions were sealed.

And forgiven.

His past five years were not sealed. He was guilty. And, he knew he was forgiven, yes, by God. By everyone else, including himself, not so much.

Someone older and definitely more seasoned than Office Miller entered the room, sat behind a desk, turned to his computer and brought up a page that Jesse couldn't see. The man didn't close the office door.

Finally, even though his computer was on, he pulled out a small notebook and said, "I'm Captain Dan Decker. Sam's filled me in on why you're here."

Without being asked, Eva handed over her paper. She'd finished filling it in while Jesse had been convincing himself that he was forgiven.

"I heard your dad broke a toe," Captain Decker said.

"A drunk ran over his foot."

Captain Decker nodded. "Mr. Campbell, you finished filling out your form?"

Jesse shook his head. Decker didn't even blink, just started talking. "We're going to build a time line. So, Mr. Campbell, tell me the first time you saw the blue 2008 Chevy Cavalier."

"On July 7, at 10:32 a.m. I was standing at the back gate of Florence State Prison, expecting to leave by the van. Instead my mother showed up in that car to pick me up."

"Completely unexpected?"

"Yes, the guard can testify to that." Jesse supplied the guard's name as well as Mike Hamm's, who'd been supposed to pick him up.

Captain Decker typed something on the computer and made a notation in his notebook. "Did your mother seem nervous? Was she looking in the rearview mirror or anything like that?"

Jesse glanced at Eva. He could play the privacy card and get rid of her so she wasn't privy to all his dirty laundry, or he could lay everything out. She knew his present but not his past. Was it better to keep it that way? However, considering the answer he was about to give, he needed her.

"She *was* nervous and looking in the rearview mirror often, but she had my five-year-old son in the backseat and was about to introduce me to him for the first time."

"And that would have made her nervous?"

"I didn't even know I had a son."

Never, of all the times he'd been pulled in, had any of his responses surprised his interrogator. Even now, Captain Decker's only visible reaction was the way his fingers paused over his notepad for a moment and his eyes sought Jesse's.

"So your mother," Captain Decker glanced over at the computer, "Susan Campbell, unexpectedly picked you up at prison—in a stolen car—for the sole purpose of introducing you to a son you didn't know existed."

"Yes."

"Did she say where or when she'd gotten the car?"

Jesse explained the story his mother had given about Matilda. The captain asked a few follow-up questions about Matilda, but Jesse had to admit that he didn't know many of the answers. He hadn't known her for long, and hadn't seen her in years. He didn't even know how she'd managed to find his mother, or why she'd known when Jesse himself was scheduled to be released from prison.

"And how did you come to be in possession of the vehicle?"

"When we arrived at the Miner's Lamp restaurant, she made me aware of Timmy in the backseat. We all went in to eat. After about twenty-five minutes, she excused herself to take a phone call, and as soon as she was outside, she took off. Apparently, on the back of a motorcycle. She left the car keys on the table."

"I can vouch for that," Eva spoke up. "I was there that day at the Miner's Lamp and saw the whole thing. He was seated in the middle of the restaurant with his family. I was sitting by the window. I heard his mother say she had a phone call. The restaurant was pretty empty, so I could hear every word whether I wanted to or not." She shot Jesse a guilty look. "I watched her go outside. I'm the one who called Jane de la Rosa over and told her that Jesse's mother had driven away with some guy on a motorcycle."

"Any idea why?" Captain Decker asked.

Jesse explained, "She didn't want the responsibility of Timmy and didn't want to risk any possibility that I'd refuse to take him."

"Has your mother ever stolen a car before?"

"You have her police record at your fingertips," Jesse pointed out.

Captain Decker didn't even blink. "Have you ever stolen a car before?"

Beside him, Eva sat up a little straighter. Her body language shouted that she expected him to say yes, and he hated it. He was better than the man he'd been.

"If anyone is in Christ, he is a new creation; the old has gone, the new has come."

"You know the answer to that, too," Jesse said. "And, if you check the record, you'll see that I admitted stealing the car. I didn't lie back then, and I won't lie today. I had no idea the Cavalier was stolen."

Captain Decker's expression didn't change. "Did it strike you odd that there was no proof of insurance, no registration, in the car? Or did you remove it?"

"I noticed the lack of both types of documents, but I wasn't surprised that they were missing. Both require the person in possession of the vehicle to pay money."

Officer Miller came to the door. "Captain, I just got off the phone with the guard at Florence State Prison. He backed up Campbell's story that the mother showed up unexpectedly and that she'd been driving a blue Cavalier. He says Campbell wasn't thrilled to see her."

See you soon.

Jesse shifted uncomfortably, though he was relieved to hear that the guard had been honest enough to back up his statement.

Officer Miller continued, "I got ahold of Jane de la Rosa, too. She says the same thing as Eva. Campbell came in with an older woman and the boy. Jane says that Eva told her the woman had run off, and that when they informed Campbell, both she and Eva watched as he ran after her and then came back in, some time after, he gathered up everything on the table, paid the bill and left."

"To meet my father about a job," Eva added.

For the next hour, it was a back-and-forth of questions and answers. Eva was like a guard dog, taking up for Jesse. It was a bit disconcerting, made him feel like he was indebted.

Again.

Decker contacted the lawyer who had agreed to take Jesse's case and solidify his custody of Timmy and then a private investigator who'd already started a search for Matilda, who apparently had no police record. He wrote things down longhand but also played with the computer. Seven Matilda Scotts had Facebook pages; none were Jesse's Matilda Scott. Decker also managed to find a phone number for Jesse's mother: disconnected.

"Before she arrived at Florence, how long had it been since you'd last seen your mother?" Captain Decker asked.

Jesse swallowed. He knew the answer because he'd figured it out the first night as he lay in the dark of a tiny two-room apartment and listened to the sound of his son breathing.

"Seven years, two months and six days."

"It's a strange twist of events, wouldn't you say?" Decker asked, standing up, clearly letting them know this meeting was over.

"What?"

"Well, for most of your life you were abandoned by her. Now your son is going through the same thing."

"There's a difference," Jesse said. "My mom abandoned me for the first time when I was five. My son Timmy's five, and he'll never be abandoned again. Not if I have any say. No one I love will ever be abandoned."

Chapter Ten

The alarm, a wind-up left by some previous occupant, sounded. Jesse groaned. Sunday, according to everyone he'd spoken to, was an easy day. No guest activities were planned until evening, and the horses were given the day off. Jacob Hubrecht, Harold said, strongly believed in family and church. From eight until two, very little was done at the ranch—the exceptions would be dealing with emergencies such as an ailing horse, if and when they occurred.

Jesse's clock read five. He, however, had hours of work ahead just to make sure the horses were taken care of.

He checked on Timmy. The boy had taken two blankets, an old sheet and three towels to create a fort using the back of the couch, a kitchen chair and two end tables. Someone, probably Eva, had given him a sleeping bag, and now Timmy had his own private area. Jesse very much wanted to leave it untouched—he remembered needing and longing for a private space when he'd been younger—but Timmy hid food in there, which Jesse had to pick through to make sure nothing was going bad. He left items such as a bowl of popcorn and cleaned up items such as smushed grapes.

This morning, as always, Timmy was buried in the sleeping bag, almost every inch hidden.

Next, Jesse got dressed and silently made his way downstairs. He'd relaxed some since that first day when he'd been so unwilling to leave Timmy alone even for a minute. Now Timmy knew enough to get dressed on his own and come find Jesse after he woke up. Jesse hoped the boy slept until eight. As much as Jesse was coming to love the boy—and he was—it still felt odd to have a small being shadowing his every move. It felt even stranger to have to offer parental guidance. Jesse had no clue if he was managing to do anything right. Was it okay for Timmy to draw stick figures with guns? Yeah, yeah, Eva pointed out they were *Star Wars* clones, but did that make it all right? Was it okay for Timmy to ride on the quad with Eva? Was it okay for Timmy to sleep in his clothes?

Both Harold and Jacob were already busy out in the field. Jesse and another wrangler stayed in the stable and began cleaning and feeding. The other wrangler talked about music and girls. Jesse nodded without really listening, all the while having Timmy foremost on his mind. Yesterday, when they got back to the ranch after Jesse was interrogated, Timmy was sucking his thumb. He'd not completely stopped in the six days that Jesse'd been in his life, but sometimes, Timmy had been so occupied, so almost content, that he forgot he even had a thumb.

The thumb hadn't left his mouth since yesterday evening.

Jesse hurried from one stall to another, talking to the horses. He wanted to return to the apartment and shower before getting Timmy up and changed. Today, they were going to church with the Hubrechts. Jesse had wished that he'd be driving the Chevy, be independent, but it sat broken and red-tagged where he'd parked it the day he arrived. One more piece of his life at a standstill.

At eight-thirty, he towel-dried his hair and then got down on his hands and knees in front of his son's fort.

"Timmy, time to get up."

No movement.

He'd learned the second morning not to touch Timmy. The fort would come down like a house built on sand—and if that happened, Timmy would be under the kitchen table for hours.

"Timmy, we're going to church. Have you ever been to church?"

No movement.

Remembering the advice Eva had passed along from her sister the previous day, Jesse told Timmy exactly what was happening. "Timmy, in twenty-five minutes we're meeting Eva and Jacob, getting in the big blue truck with them and heading into town for church. Jacob will be driving. Eva will be on the passenger side. You and I will be in back. Once we get to church, we will sit in a pew and learn about God. Then, afterward, we'll come back here, and I thought maybe we'd go to the pool. What will not happen today, I promise you, is that we'll be separated. Now, I'm going in the bedroom to get dressed. I've left your clothes on the couch. I need you to get dressed, too."

Jesse started to move away from the fort, then stopped as a new thought occurred to him. Leaning down, he whispered, "Timmy, did you have an accident?" Ever since the first night, Jesse had made sure Timmy wore pull-ups when he went to sleep, but sometimes the pull-ups weren't enough.

Two minutes later, Jesse had Eva on her cell phone.

"I need Timmy hosed down."

Instead of Timmy going to the back door of the dining hall, Eva came to them. When the door of the truck opened, and one leg edged out, Jesse knew he was in trouble. As the rest of her emerged, his heart almost stopped. It was an Eva Jesse'd not seen before. Gone were the jeans topped by a colorful shirt. And today *clean* and *soft* were inadequate to describe her. *Stunning* and *curvy* were more accurate.

He'd never seen anyone quite like her. A solid shimmering green shirt hugged her torso, emphasizing that she was definitely a vibrant woman. A necklace of silver and turquoise, clearly Native American in design, hung around her neck. Her skirt was ankle-length of soft brown material. Her boots matched her shirt. He'd not been aware they even made green boots.

Wow.

Jesse swallowed, suddenly dry-mouthed.

Timmy, forehead wrinkled and head bowed, came through the barn and stood by a wheelbarrow that Jesse had neglected to put away.

"Hey, Timmy," Eva greeted him.

Jesse tried not to care that she didn't seem to notice him.

"There's a hose in the back," she said. "Let's head there."

Jesse started to tell her there was a hose inside the stable, but then he remembered that she didn't like the stable, didn't like horses.

In just ten minutes, she had Timmy hosed down. She did it without fuss, without getting dirty and without making Timmy feel like he was anything but the most important person on earth. Jesse would almost be willing to fake an accident himself if it meant she'd treat him the way she treated Timmy.

The Apache Creek church boasted a congregation of just over a hundred. Eva and her family had attended all their lives. Her dad was an elder. As she stepped from the truck, she looked back to see what Jesse and Timmy were doing. Both were sitting in the back, not moving.

"You coming in?"

Jesse didn't answer right away, and Eva got the impression that he was praying. Never had she met such a complex man. A moment later, he exited the truck, helped Timmy down and followed her dad inside the church. Eva started to bring up the rear but heard, "Eva!"

Jane de la Rosa hurried to her side. "What happened yesterday? Sam Miller had me on the phone for almost an hour. I told him twice what you and I went through on Monday. Did they find out who stole the car? Is Jesse in trouble?"

"We think his ex-girlfriend—Timmy's mom—stole the car. Her name's Matilda Scott. Sam's trying to hunt her down, and Jesse's mother, too. But neither have what you call a permanent address. I don't think Jesse's in real trouble."

"Sam and some other cop came down to the

restaurant yesterday evening. I heard them talking to my boss about our security cameras."

"Track Susan through the motorcycle," Eva exclaimed. "What a great idea!"

"Yes," Jane agreed. "Ideally, they'll see Jesse's mother driving the blue Chevy and parking at the restaurant."

"As well as leaving on the back of a motorcycle with a visible license plate."

Entering the church, Eva turned toward an adult classroom while Jane hurried down the hall to help with the first through third grades.

Was Timmy in a children's class?

No, he was sitting in the back of the adult classroom next to Jesse. He was looking at his thumbs and wiggling a bit. Nobody had thought to bring paper and pencils. Eva half smiled. Just Timmy's luck to wind up in an environment ruled by adults.

She sat on the other side of the room, next to a family she'd grown up with. When Bible class was over, she found Jane, and both of them sat in the back of the auditorium.

"Why don't you invite Jesse to sit with us?" Jane asked.

"Because for the past six days, I've seen him every day. I need space."

"He is cute."

Eva didn't respond. Mostly because she agreed, but also because every ex-con they'd helped out, except for one, had either been arrested again while working for them or disappeared into the night.

It had been only six days, but already Eva was dreading Jesse's disappearance.

The Lost and Found closet contained many things for Jesse to borrow. But people who left things behind usually left the things because they were ugly.

The exception being things for children.

Timmy found a perfectly normal pair of Spider-Man swim trunks. If they had been a little bigger, Jesse would have claimed them for himself. The only pair of grown male swim trunks were bright purple with big yellow flowers on them.

They had to have been someone's gag gift.

Jesse, however, intended on keeping his word even if he looked like a buff orchid while doing it. He'd told Timmy they'd go swimming. Words were the only thing he had to offer right now. He couldn't buy his son a bike or a video game player or anything like that. He had one paycheck in his wallet and would soon owe money to a lawyer he hadn't met. But he'd told his son they'd go swimming together, and that was exactly what they were going to do.

Sunday passed with a full day of play—not only in the pool but also back in the apartment, where he and Timmy played seventeen games of Go Fish.

First thing Jesse noticed was how hard it was for Timmy to play in the pool and suck his thumb at the same time. Go Fish had no such limitation. When the sun finally started going down, Jesse and Timmy had dinner and then did a bed check, making sure all the horses had water and were comfortable. Back in the apartment, both settled on the couch and turned on the television. Jesse slipped in a Scooby-Doo DVD, again from Lost and Found, and leaned back, falling asleep before the first Scooby snack.

He woke up at ten minutes after five the following morning. For once, Timmy wasn't in his fort. Instead, he was sound asleep on the couch, his head on Jesse's knee. The television droned on. It had switched off the DVD player when the movie ended, and now the morning news told of gloom.

Jesse gently rearranged Timmy and went to get dressed. Today he started his second week at the Lost Dutchman. He was contributing more, both with the horses and the guests. He knew which horse to give a beginner or an expert, and which would allow the step stool for riders who needed assistance. He knew that when Eva took trail ride reservations, she asked questions, wrote down key bits of information and passed them on to the wranglers. They'd find out beforehand who was scared, who was experienced and who had bad knees. Her organized efficiency made his job—and his life—easier in so many ways.

Two hours later, he headed toward the main building. He found Eva at the front desk, her fingers dancing over a keyboard and her face scrunched up as she frowned at the screen. She was back to her normal attire. Today she wore a black-and-red swirled top, black jeans and black cowboy boots.

He liked the skirt she'd worn to church better, but only just.

"I need to go to town later today. What does the Lost Dutchman do for guests who don't have vehicles?"

"Nothing. We don't have a van, although it's on my dream list. People who come in from out of town usually rent a car. A few times, I've done an airport pickup, or Harold has. Where do you need to go?"

"Personal business. Never mind. I'll figure something out. Oh, by the way, a man named Trevor Winslow should be here soon. Send him down to the dining hall when he arrives, will you?"

Stepping out into the sunshine, Jesse saw Timmy hurrying up the road. He was dressed, and his eyes had the pinched look of "Is my father still here?" but he was moving faster than he had a week ago. He no longer acted like an old man who had to be forced from the couch to the table to the stairs.

"You hungry?" Jesse asked.

Timmy nodded.

Everyone who wanted to go on a ride was out. The horses were cared for. Breakfast at the Lost Dutchman was next on the list. Mondays were blueberry pancakes, scrambled eggs and bacon. Timmy took three pancakes and nothing else. Jesse took three of everything. He'd just managed one bite when Trevor Winslow came into the dining room. Eva was on the man's heels, her mouth moving and her hands flying with every word, as if she were still in front of the computer.

Waving Trevor over, Jesse stood and waited to shake the man's hand. Eva'd turned off and headed for the kitchen. She soon came out with a plate laden with food. For a moment, Jesse worried that she'd sit down with them. But she didn't. She merely said, "If there's anything else you need, let me know."

"You've got quite a fan," Trevor said after she left.

"Which is surprising, considering what's been going on since I arrived," Jesse said, quickly filling Trevor in on the first encounter with Eva at the Miner's Lamp and ending with their three-hour stay at Apache Creek's police station.

"Even the guard at Florence vouched for me. At this point, I don't think I'm their suspect."

"Good thing."

For the next thirty minutes, Trevor asked questions about the ranch and what Jesse was doing there. Then Jacob came in and joined them. "Trevor, good to see you."

"You, too, Jacob. Jesse tells me he's adjusting to his living arrangements and the community. Things are going fine?"

"They are. He's a natural. I've got him giving lessons. He's even giving them to two boys from town. It keeps them out of trouble, and he's doing a fine job with them. He's one of my best intuitive hands. He knows, after only a week, which horse he should assign a student, and he doesn't rush into the lesson. He takes time to let the horse meet the student."

Trevor gave a half smile.

"You ride?" Jesse asked.

"Last time I rode," Trevor said, "I put a quarter in a slot and got a whole minute."

Jacob guffawed. "We need to get you on a horse. Jesse, which one should it be?"

"I'd say Cinderella."

"Perfect," Jacob agreed.

Trevor stopped the conversation with a "Not today. I've got two more visits to make." It was enough to remind Jesse why Trevor was here. Before moving away, Jacob told Trevor about the Friday night drunk and his broken toe.

After Jacob left, Trevor spoke to Timmy. "Are you learning to ride?"

Timmy nodded.

"Who's teaching you?"

Timmy pointed to Jacob's retreating form and then to Jesse.

"Are you happy here?"

Timmy nodded.

Jesse's heart swelled. He'd never felt anything like it. And all because his son was happy, with him, here.

"I have an appointment with the lawyer you recommended," Jesse said. "It's this afternoon. If there's any cost later, he's agreed to let me make payments over time. I need to prove Timmy's my son, get the paperwork, so I can start getting him some help and get him in school next month."

Trevor stood. "Sounds like you're doing the best you can. Offhand, I can't think of anyone on my caseload who exited prison and became a surprise single father the same day. You've got your work cut out for you."

Jesse stood, too, and looked down at Timmy. "I'm a hard worker."

A hollow, empty feeling followed Jesse as he walked Trevor around the stable and arena. He then took his parole officer upstairs to the apartment and showed him how they lived. Funny, until this moment he'd thought the apartment was just right. Now it looked incredibly small. Trevor didn't seem to care and glanced inside the newly washed and reestablished fort before commenting to Timmy, "You need a flashlight. I had a fort when I was just a few grades older than you are. I'd crawl in and read. You like to read?"

Timmy shrugged.

After what felt like hours, but had been only one, Jesse and Timmy escorted Trevor to the main building. Trevor stayed long enough to watch Eva hose Timmy down. Then he drove off, leaving Jesse wondering how long he'd feel like Big Brother was watching.

If only Jesse had a big brother. As it was, he had so much to do and no one to help. No family.

Eva came to stand on the porch. She shaded her eyes with her hand and watched as Trevor drove away. "It was a good first visit. I've been praying about it."

How many similar visits had she witnessed?

Enough to have an opinion, but then Miss Eva Hubrecht had an opinion about everything.

She'd been praying?

That was something he should have been doing more of, because one of the first scripture verses Mike had thrown Jesse's way read "The Lord watches over you—the Lord is your shade at your right hand."

It was the nudge Jesse needed just now. He

might not have family to watch over him, but he had God watching over him, and he had Timmy to watch over.

Jesse followed Eva back to the lobby. "I need to get into town and find the bus schedule or something. I have some errands to run today."

"I've started the paperwork to add you to our insurance so you can use the ranch trucks. It will take a few days. In the meantime, I can take you into town and drop you off where you want to go. We don't really have a city bus because we're too small. There are a few shuttles, privately owned, but those don't come out this far and will cost you."

One of the items on Jesse's list was opening a bank account. Until then, he just had a paycheck and wasn't willing to pay a fee to cash it. "I'd appreciate the ride. I have an appointment at Kildare and Sons at eleven. Can you get me there?"

"I'll drive down to the stables and pick you and Timmy up at ten-thirty. It's mostly my free day, too, and I always go to the Miner's Lamp for lunch. You can call me when you're done."

He remembered seeing her there his first day in town. She'd been at a table with a book and a wary expression.

At least she was no longer wary.

An hour later, *he* was.

The lawyer's office was a remodeled fast-food restaurant. However, no expense had been spared in the renovation. Dark wood paneling graced the waiting room. Fresh flowers were in the middle, and the tables held magazines about politics and finance. It appeared to Jesse that Timmy looked at the end tables first. None were big enough for him to crawl under. Most looked like they'd come from a museum and shouldn't be touched.

Jesse gave his name to the receptionist. She handed him a clipboard, just like on the first day he'd visited his PO, and said, "Mr. Kildare will see you shortly."

Jesse filled out the form, careful to make his handwriting legible. Never before had he cared whether or not his writing was discernible. "This is our first step," he told Timmy. "I know I'm your father, but we have to prove it to everyone else since your mother is not around."

Timmy looked at his feet.

A memory stirred, something from Jesse's past. He'd just been left with an aunt who'd shouted after his mother, "You better not leave him for long!"

Her name had been Bonnie. She'd been older than his mother and had three kids of her own. Her husband had been displeased, very displeased, with Jesse's appearance.

Jesse'd been about Timmy's age.

"You miss your mother?" Jesse asked.

Timmy nodded.

Before Jesse could ask any more questions, the

receptionist called his name. Soon Jesse sat before a desk bigger than the bed he slept in. Classical music played softly in the background.

"Is there anything that the boy shouldn't hear?" Peter Kildare asked.

"No, he already knows anything that we have to talk about."

Kildare opened a folder and skimmed the papers inside, but Jesse got the idea he'd already read the history and was skimming it for effect. Finally Kildare cleared his throat and said, "I've never had a case quite like yours. You've been out of prison a week, and you've had sole custody all that time. But Matilda Scott didn't turn the boy over to you?"

"No, she turned him over to my mother, who showed up at the prison gate." Jesse shared the whole story, leaving nothing out, including both Eva's and Jane's participation, then having to beg Jacob Hubrecht for a job, and ending with the stolen vehicle and his time at the police station on Saturday.

Kildare didn't even blink. "And you're sure you want to pursue paternity?"

"I've never been more sure of anything in my life."

"My private investigator found your mother." Kildare pushed over a piece of paper with a phone number on it. "She was pretty defensive until she realized the car she'd left with you was stolen. Then she started answering questions."

"You find out anything?" Jesse asked.

"Just what you'd already told us on the phone. But now that the police are looking for Matilda, it will help your paternity case."

"What do you mean?"

"The process will go a whole lot smoother, a whole lot quicker and a whole lot cheaper, if she's there to sign the paperwork and work with you instead of you doing all this alone."

In the past week, Jesse had not once considered Matilda working with him.

"Plus," Kildare continued, "during paternity testing, it's best to have a sample from the mother so that the lab can trace the remaining genetic markers to you."

"And that will be proof?"

"It's a step in the right direction. Without Matilda, there's less information to go on." Kildare called his secretary in. Together they arranged for Timmy to be seen by a local pediatrician and also a child psychologist.

"We want to prove that you're doing everything to make sure Timmy's taken care of."

For the next twenty minutes, Kildare went on about the Office of Vital Records, affidavit acknowledgment and legal guardianship. Apparently without it, Timmy couldn't provide a sample and be tested.

"I'm also keeping the private detective on the case," Kildare said. "We need to find Miss Scott. Right now, she's the only one who can authorize release of Timmy's medical history. We contacted the hospital where he was born, but all we can prove is that there was a healthy birth. We have no idea if he was born mute or if that came later. Given that he doesn't talk, we need her permission and soon."

It gave Jesse pause. If Matilda came back into the picture, what if she denied that Timmy was his?

Or worse, what if she wanted to take Timmy back?

Chapter Eleven

The next morning, it was very clear to Eva that Jesse Campbell was on edge. At breakfast he kept looking over his shoulder as if expecting someone to jump out of the shadows.

He glared at the other hands and sat at a table alone with Timmy. That wasn't strange in itself, but usually there was a little morning banter between him and the other men even if they didn't sit together.

She shouldn't be concerned.

Except he might scare the guests.

Glancing around the dining hall, she realized that she was the only one who noticed Jesse's mood.

It's not my place to step in, just because he's in a mood, she reminded herself. *I didn't want him here in the first place.*

Yet, hadn't Dad said that she needed to work

on being understanding? Well, she had come in here to eat breakfast before tackling the wedding the Lost Dutchman would be hosting in just four days. Settling down next to Timmy and across from Jesse, she said, "You're here early."

"Couldn't sleep." He kept his attention on his plate and not on her. She waited, but it soon became apparent he wasn't going to share anything else.

"Dad changed the schedule. We've added a few more lessons for townies. He thinks you can handle them."

He rearranged some of the hash browns on his plate. "I saw."

Two-word responses weren't getting her anyplace. "Want to tell me what's going on?"

"What do you mean?" This time he looked at her, a let's-get-this-over-with expression on his face.

"Since you've arrived, Timmy's not willingly let you out of his sight. You've been pushing him away like a mother bird, telling him to come to me for his morning hose-down, wanting him to play on the playground while you work in the arena, et cetera. This morning, however, it's you who won't let him out of your sight. What happened yesterday when you went to see the lawyer? Did he say Timmy could be taken away from you? Is that why you're watching him like a hawk?"

Jesse again rearranged the hash browns on his plate. Timmy followed his example.

"Come on, Jesse, who else are you going to talk to? I don't think there's anything in this battle I haven't been privy to. Oh, and by the way, do you realize this is the first breakfast you haven't said a prayer for first?"

Now he frowned, his mind momentarily off whatever was bothering him. Timmy raised an eyebrow.

"Let's bow our heads," Jesse said before uttering the shortest prayer Eva'd ever heard.

Right when he ended, Cook came out the swinging kitchen doors and put a plate in front of Eva. "Didn't look like you were going to fix your own."

Eva thanked him, picked up her fork and started rearranging her own hash browns. Cook looked at the three of them and shook his head before returning to his duties.

After the third hash brown creation, she said, "I can do this as long as you can. And both of us need to get back to work with good attitudes."

"You don't need to be bothered with this," Jesse said.

"It affects your performance here. My dad is thrilled with what you're doing. And since he has a broken toe, quite honestly, we need you in top form. Maybe I can help. Or at least take whatever questions you have to my sister. She gives pretty good advice."

Jesse finally took a bite of his breakfast. Then he began. "The lawyer says that without Matilda giving DNA and signing paperwork, we're going to have quite a few roadblocks to having me recognized as Timmy's father. The big one is that without her genetic markers, we'll have a less informative result from the paternity test. And we can't even test Timmy until we have a legal guardian, which I'm not."

"That's a question my sister can help with. I'll call her today."

"The other thing," he admitted, "is I want to start looking for Matilda. But if I go looking for the people we hung around with, well, they might be known felons. Talking with them could hurt my rehabilitation."

"I'll ask Elise about that, too."

It took ten more minutes for Jesse to tell her everything he was worried about. His problems with finding Timmy's medical history were at the top of his list, followed by worries about a visit planned next Monday to a child psychologist.

Jesse's pager went off then. He checked it and said, "I've got a trail ride scheduled. I do appreciate the help with Timmy."

Timmy stood, following Jesse's example. The

two of them carried their plates over to the dishwasher window and then headed out the back door.

She'd see Timmy in a couple of hours. He'd want to be hosed off. Then, she'd see Jesse tonight. She was a bit uncomfortable with how much she looked forward to the attention.

Not that it was anything but work-related.

Three hours later, she left the computer and headed through the kitchen. She snatched a cookie from the sheet Cook had left to cool and went to wait on the back porch. It was about time for Timmy's hosing.

Standing outside, she noted everything going on. The pool had at least ten people in it. Not bad for a slow Tuesday. The old schoolhouse that they used for kids' crafts looked to have two kids. Patti was in there, supervising the kids while they painted popsicle stick horses. The playground and tennis court were empty. This time of the day, no one was on a ride.

Yet one of their new lessons had scheduled an afternoon time slot. Patti had taken the reservation; given the unbearable heat at that time of day, Eva figured Patti should have tried to talk the woman out of it.

Of course, now that Eva could see Jesse in the arena giving directions to the woman, Eva knew exactly why the last-minute lesson had been scheduled.

"Something to watch, huh?" Her father came to stand next to her, still favoring the foot with the broken toe.

"We've added two new lessons, both to females in their twenties, and both are willing to bake in the afternoon sun for the opportunity to have Jesse be the one to teach them. I'm thinking that certain females were paying attention to something besides the sermon last Sunday."

Her father nodded. "It's a small town, and there are not that many available men. About time Sam Miller got some competition. Look at that. Daisy's feeling her oats today."

"Her gash all better?"

"The vet said she's good to go." Jacob chuckled. "Maybe a little too good. Jesse might have put Crystal on one of the other quarter horses."

"I don't think Crystal cares what horse she rides." The woman was paying much more attention to Jesse's toned physique as he talked her through the lesson. Additionally, she'd probably also noticed the way Jesse treated Timmy. To an outsider who didn't know the whole situation, Jesse looked like the perfect single father with a well-behaved son.

The woman taking the lesson was none other than Crystal Glenn. Until two years ago, she'd lived with her parents in a big house that had horse property. She'd never been in Elise or Emily's league, but she knew how to sit a horse and had even been in a few competitions. What she didn't know was how to rope in a member of the male persuasion.

"Watch," her father urged. "She's being sassy."

"You sure you mean the horse?"

Her father didn't catch the innuendo. Instead, he said, somewhat in awe, "See how Jesse keeps bringing the rider back to halting, then trotting, then halting? It's exactly what the mare needs. We've had Mitch working for us two summers now, and he'd have lost control of both Daisy and the rider by now. I made a good decision bringing Jesse here."

"We can't afford him." Funny, this time her words sounded half-hearted.

"He's working for the minimum."

"He can't afford to do that for long. He'll have lawyer fees, doctor bills, and once Timmy gets registered for school, there will be one necessity after another that he'll need to buy."

"You've been talking to Elise again?"

"Elise is offering Jesse some sound advice. He needs it. I'm trying to talk her into coming for a visit."

Her father didn't acknowledge Eva's words, but Eva knew how he really felt. His second-born, Elise, was the most like him of his three daughters. She was the horsewoman of the family, easily traversing through gymkhanas, Little Britches and Junior Rodeos, racking up buckles and titles in barrel racing and roping. Four years ago she'd been talking about future World Championships. Then her best friend died, and Elise had blamed herself. She'd been too busy practicing to check her texts. She'd missed the early morning call for help. By the time she read Cindy's text that said, B is drunk. Cm gt me. I dnt want 2 b with him. We @ the rodeo grounds and called the police, Cindy was dead.

Elise had pretty much buried herself saving others since then, turning her back on her fiancé, her family and the arena.

Jacob didn't understand the path Elise had taken, and Eva didn't know what to say. She didn't understand her sister's choices any more than her dad did. All Eva knew was how much she had envied the abilities that Elise had left behind. The Lost Dutchman was a horse ranch. Everyone rode, from family to employees to guests. Elise had been the queen of it all; Eva was the lone holdout.

Even Cook, who didn't get excited about anything, occasionally took a morning ride and then returned as if edified.

How could Elise walk away?

"I'm gonna take him to the Doin's Rodeo over in Payson next month," Jacob broke the silence.

"What? Why?"

Her father seemed surprised at the question. He looked from Jesse to Eva and back to Jesse.

In a heartbeat, Eva knew the answer to her question. He missed going to the rodeo with someone who might be as excited about the event as he was. The few times Eva had gone, she never left the merchandise area. She had more I'm a Cowgirl shirts than anyone else. Eva's youngest sister, Emily, loved the rodeo, too, and had competed in some. But participating wasn't her calling, and she wasn't a very good spectator. No, she'd rather sidle up to a Native American competitor and get his story. She'd do the same if there happened to be a Native American running the Ferris wheel. She cared more about the history of the event, the people, than the competition.

Sometimes her dad lassoed Harold into attending. But while her dad longed for the days when he'd traveled the circuit, Harold just grumbled about choices.

Eva knew about choices, too. Get on the horse or stay safe on the ground. And if she wanted to run the Lost Dutchman ranch someday, she needed to get over her fear of horses.

Jesse knew he had an audience, in addition to Timmy. On the back porch of the main house, both Eva and her father stood watching him.

Jacob, he knew, had plans for him. He'd mentioned some rodeo over in Payson, just for fun. Jesse wasn't sure if he remembered what fun was.

"Am I doing this right?" Crystal Glenn asked. She was maybe twenty and definitely single. She'd told him that last detail twice.

"Doing what right?" Jesse had no clue what she wanted to know. She'd asked for an intermediate lesson, but it was obvious she was advanced. She knew how to sit a horse, how to walk, trot, canter and probably how to gallop and jump.

"My posture? Is it right?"

Her back had been straight when she'd asked the question, but now that he studied her, she slumped a little, and the hand that gripped the reins grew slack.

"You can sit up more and—"

She popped up like she'd just been plugged in. Her smile was extra bright—and so were her clothes. She wore what looked like a brand-new white sleeveless shirt topping a pair of red capri pants. She was smarter than he was, actually. He wore jeans, and last time he'd heard, the Arizona temperature was pushing one hundred ten. Her hair was cut short, maybe too short, and her expression was eager. At first he'd thought she was eager for a lesson. Now he got the idea that the lesson was a ruse and he was the real target.

"That's fine," he said. "Go ahead and bend your knee a little more."

She did, a lot more.

He was better with kids. He'd sure enjoyed the lesson with the eight-year-old this morning. That kid hung on Jesse's every suggestion. This woman hung on Jesse's every word, whether the words were directed at her or not. She'd nodded enthusiastically every time he said something to Timmy, whether it be a direction—"Don't walk Pinocchio so close to the client"—or a suggestion—"Why don't you go find Eva? It's time for your shower."

Right now, just like Crystal, Timmy was sitting straight up and had his knees bent. He looked ridiculous.

Jesse wished that Timmy could manage to look eager, just once, whether it was for riding Pinocchio or playing twenty games of Go Fish. Lately, Jesse'd seen a few glimmers of what Timmy could look like behind his mask of indifference. Glancing back at Jacob and Eva, Jesse got the idea they knew exactly why Crystal was there—and they knew how uncomfortable Jesse was.

"Sure," he muttered to himself, "stay up there instead of coming down and helping."

At that moment, his gaze locked with Eva's.

Just like at the restaurant. That day, he'd sensed judgment in her expression. Right now, he noted a certain reservation, as if she were afraid to show him too much of who she was.

"You want me to gallop? I can, you know. We don't have to stay in the arena. We can—"

"I never leave the arena during a first lesson." It was true, but it was also an excuse. Crystal Glenn was only his third client. The other two, the eight-year-old boy and his mother, were so novice that they didn't want to leave the arena.

"But—"

"Just tighten up the rein and bring your knees a little more to the front."

If Eva felt vulnerable, how did she think Jesse felt? He didn't like relying on a female. They had a way of letting you down.

"I don't like holding my knees this close to the front," Crystal complained.

"Find where you're comfortable."

And she did, with ease, convincing Jesse that in the world of horses, she knew more than he did, and this was one more feminine farce.

One he had to live with because it was his job.

What bothered him most was knowing that he wanted Eva to come down and put an end the farce. Instead, with a flip of that long blond hair, she turned and sashayed back into the house. The show was over, for her. She could change the channel; he couldn't. He still had twenty-five minutes of an hour-long lesson to go.

After what seemed like hours, the session ended,

and Crystal easily swung her right leg over the saddle and dismounted.

"I can't believe how much I've forgotten," she gushed. "I should have signed up for lessons long ago."

Those pronouncements were followed by chatter that told him what she did for a living—nurse; how far away she lived—just down from the church; and what she liked doing for fun—go to the movies. She mentioned a kid-friendly one showing this weekend. The suggestion was followed by a hopeful smile in Timmy's direction.

Jesse looked over to see that Timmy and Pinocchio were standing completely still. Timmy stared at his hands, and Pinocchio was asleep.

"We've got a big wedding here this weekend. I'll be doing double-duty. Movies just aren't my thing right now." He nudged Daisy toward the gate.

"I can help with Daisy," Crystal offered, following.

"I'm going to loosen the cinch and walk her for a bit. You go ahead and talk to Eva about what you want to do next."

She opened her mouth and then shut it again. Wisely she said, "We'll talk more next time."

As she headed for the gate to the arena, Jesse noted that she knew how to sashay, too, but she wasn't nearly as gifted as Eva.

Since Daisy wasn't puffing, Jesse knew she

really didn't need cooling down, but he wasn't about to let go of the excuse that got him out of Crystal's company. He led her across the arena, careful to walk slowly enough not to catch Crystal's attention. That was all he needed—some town girl thinking he was the catch of the day. He'd almost made it to the gate when he heard a shout. Looking up at the main house, he saw Eva standing on the back porch, pointing at him and waving frantically. He let go of Daisy's lead rope and started to move to the gate but realized Eva was pointing behind him, even as she ran down to her ATV and jumped on.

He turned, seeing nothing unusual, just the arena, the dirt, Pinocchio still standing still, sleeping—

Riderless.

Never, not even when he'd heard the gunshot meaning something had gone wrong with Billy's convenience store robbery, had Jesse felt such panic. From where he was standing, he could see Timmy's head on the ground, his shoulders in the dirt, but the rest of his body leaned against the pony because Timmy's foot was still in the stirrup!

If the pony moved, Timmy could be dragged.

Jesse didn't run. No way did he want to spook Pinocchio, but in four steps—each to the beat of his mental prayers saying *dear God, please God,* he made it to the pony and steadied the animal with one hand to its flank.

"It's okay, girl. No need to wake up."

Behind him, he could hear the ATV coming his way and the shouts between Crystal and Eva.

"What happened?" Crystal called.

"Timmy fell."

When he got to Timmy's side, he realized that Timmy must have fallen asleep and slipped right out of the saddle. At the most, Timmy had dinged the side of his head, and he couldn't have done it very hard—not if he slept through it.

Jesse carefully removed Timmy's tennis shoe from the stirrup and then moved Timmy away from the pony. His son's skin was warm, droplets of sweat beaded on his forehead, and his shirt was damp.

"Hey, Timmy," Jesse said, caressing his forehead until Timmy opened his eyes. "You okay?"

Timmy looked around, confused. His eyes opened wider when he saw Eva and Crystal coming to a stop right above him. That got a reaction. A slow keen started.

"I think he fell asleep and then just fell off the horse," Jesse explained to the approaching women.

"I saw him go down," Eva said. "One minute he was looking at his hands, and the next minute he was tilting sideways. I can't believe he didn't wake up when he hit the ground."

"Good thing there were no rocks around," Crystal noted.

"Good thing," Eva whispered.

Something in her voice made him look up from stroking Timmy's face. It was a possibility he hadn't considered: Timmy getting hurt. Maybe because for the past week, all he'd thought about was what kind of hurt would make a five-year-old stop talking, stop looking people in the eye.

Eva looked ready to pass out.

Crystal crouched next to him and lifted Timmy up. Gone was the flirt; present was a professional nurse. "You might want to put some ice on the side of his face, though I doubt he'll let you keep it there for long."

Jesse didn't have a chance to comment or ask Crystal any questions. He was too busy watching Eva's eyes roll back in her head before she fainted dead away. He caught her before she hit the ground. Lifting her up, he looked down at Crystal bending over Timmy. "Let's get them out of the sun."

Timmy scrambled to his feet before Crystal got a hold of him. He huddled next to Jesse as they walked to the main house. Long blond hair cascaded over Jesse's arm. Eva's skin was warm, tantalizingly so. Sweat beaded on her forehead, and if he'd had a spare hand, he'd have brushed it away. The back of her shirt was damp.

He didn't mind.

It had been more than five years since he'd held a woman. And if he was honest, Eva was more woman than he'd ever held.

Later, Timmy settled on the floor in the Hubrechts' living room near Eva's loom. The yarn and colors seemed to fascinate him. Jesse watched, but Timmy didn't seem inclined to touch. Eva was lying down in her bedroom where he'd carried her, a cold cloth on her forehead.

Jacob was shaking his head at what had transpired, and all Jesse could do was wonder what had made Eva faint.

There wasn't even any blood.

"She'll be all right," Jacob said. "It's been a long time since she's been comfortable around horses."

"Why doesn't she like horses?" Jesse asked. "Everyone else does."

For a moment, he didn't think Jacob was going to answer. Then the man bowed his head and said in a low voice, "She was tossed off of one when she was in grade school. Right in that arena. Of all things, a family of turkeys made their way through the fencing and spooked Palomino Pete. I was right there immediately. She landed on a jagged rock. Still don't know how one that big made it inside the arena."

"She was all right?" Jesse asked. From what he could tell, she was perfect.

"There was an injury to her scalp." Jacob ended up at the bookcase, where he picked up one of the trophies his daughter Elise had earned. "Bled like crazy."

"And that's why she's scared of horses?"

Jacob set the trophy down and shook his head. "It was six months after we lost her mother. Car accident. We were coming back from an auction. She was in the truck about a half block ahead of me. We were both pulling horse trailers. I saw it happening. An SUV pulled in front of her. I saw the brake lights. I saw her spin out of control. The telephone pole wound up in the front seat. Naomi didn't have a chance."

Eva's mother, the woman in the picture above the dining room entrance, the first weaver. Jesse'd wondered how she died.

"When Eva got hurt, I saw the blood, and it took me right back to Naomi. No, it wasn't being thrown from the horse that put Eva off horses. It was me. I was so scared she'd get hurt again that I kept her off a horse even when she wanted to get back on. I told her over and over again that it wasn't safe, and finally she believed me. I'd like a do-over."

Jesse wanted a few of those, too.

Chapter Twelve

Eva was up and around by the next day, fully recovered, but she didn't seem inclined to talk about why she'd fainted or how she felt about Jesse carrying her to her bedroom. Every time he got near her, she remembered some wedding detail and off she went.

She was cute when she was flustered.

Cute all the time, really.

Over the next few days, Jesse couldn't stop thinking of what her father had told him about how Eva had gotten scared off of riding. Jesse didn't want that for Timmy, so he didn't stop Timmy from prepping Pinocchio for their morning ride. A few times each day, he'd see Eva standing on the back porch, watching them. He'd wave, and she'd wave back. Then she'd go inside before they rode off.

Must be hard for her to live on a dude ranch

where horses were the lifeblood and be afraid of horses.

At breakfast, or lunch, or whenever their paths crossed, she shared some tidbit her sister, the social worker, thought he should know. By the time Jesse got in to see the child psychologist, he'd have a wealth of knowledge.

Elise thought Timmy might have selective mutism because of the anxiety of everything he'd been through. Her advice was to make him feel comfortable, secure and relaxed. Jesse hoped Timmy was comfortable in his fort. As for secure and relaxed, well, Jesse didn't feel secure or relaxed, so it was hard to gauge if Timmy was.

"She give any advice on something I can actually do?" Jesse asked at breakfast on Friday. It was the first time Eva, clearly distracted, sat down with them instead of just passing their table, putting a hand on Jesse's shoulder and saying a few words before hurrying off to do something more important.

"Elise says you should keep a diary. Record every success, everything you do that moves you forward toward a goal with Timmy. Not only will it help keep you motivated, but should you have to go to court, you'll have a record of all you've done."

The biggest milestone, Jesse thought, was Timmy becoming a horse whisperer. It sure appeared that Pinocchio and Timmy could communicate. But that wasn't Jesse's doing.

Jesse wished Timmy would whisper something to him.

Come to think of it, Jesse wished Eva would whisper something to him, something sweet and tender, but that couldn't be. Jacob Hubrecht would kick Jesse off the ranch without hesitation if he thought Jesse might be having romantic thoughts about Eva. But ever since holding her in his arms, it seemed all Jesse could think of was her.

"A diary, huh?"

"For both you and Timmy."

"Hear that, Timmy? We get to keep a diary. It's where we keep track of all we do in a day."

Eva scanned some texts on her cell phone. "The bride wants to know if there are three more rooms available. This is going to be our busiest July weekend ever. We're full." She set the phone down on the table. "I don't think Elise wants you to keep track of your daily routine. She means details about your day that show growth, success."

"Give me an example," he urged her. "If you were keeping a diary like this for yourself, what would be in it?"

She stopped eating to think. After a moment, in exasperation, she said, "Everything I can think of I do all the time."

"Would booking the last three rooms be something you'd write about?"

"No, because I had nothing to do with the reservations. They're just part of the job. Now, if I'd put out a special coupon and purposely tracked the guests who came because of the coupon, that I could write down."

"Because you actually had something to do with getting the reservation."

"Right."

Jesse leaned toward her. "So, tell me five things you'd write down from yesterday."

She gave a short laugh. "Yesterday was all about the wedding. Nothing was about me."

"Nothing? Really?"

"Best example I can think of happened your first full day here."

Jesse felt oddly pleased. When Eva thought about something successful that had happened to her lately, it involved him.

"It was when I figured out how to get Timmy clean. I was pretty impressed with myself. Hosing him down was a good idea."

There went the pleased feeling. Her sense of accomplishment came out of his failure—*he* should have been the one to figure out a way to get his son clean. "Give me something from yesterday," he suggested.

She scrunched up her face, thinking. "Well, I

sold a basket to one of the wedding guests who came early."

"That happen often?" Jesse asked.

"Often enough." She looked at him. "Not special enough, huh?"

"If my goal is helping Timmy, what's your goal?"

"Keeping the Lost Dutchman in the black."

"That's your job," Jesse said. "It shouldn't be your goal. It shouldn't define you."

"It makes me happy."

Jesse thought about it for a moment. Thought about all Eva did in a day, working the front desk, helping in the dining room, organizing a wedding and even sitting before the loom, weaving a blanket so spectacular that he wanted one.

"I think your goal should be riding a horse, even if it's just around the arena once."

She sat back, staring at him with a look of dismay. Then she glanced around the dining hall as if hoping someone would rescue her. Cook was too busy tinkering with one of the food warmers. Mitch was sitting at a back table, swayed back with his feet on the chair across from him, paying no attention to Eva and Jesse.

"My goal is Timmy," Jesse finally said. "I wish it were something as easy as riding a horse."

"Easy," she whispered. Then her cell phone rang. She answered the call, tucked the phone against her ear and gathered up her breakfast dishes. Jesse watched as she went to the dishwasher window.

One thing he'd learned from the conversation—besides that he liked talking to her—was that everyone needed a goal, and sometimes the people who seemed to have it easy needed a goal the most.

Eva wasn't as happy as she pretended to be; otherwise, she wouldn't think that eating alone at the Miner's Lamp every Monday was going out.

He was still thinking about her when Friday came to a close. Everyone from the wedding party had arrived. Jacob pulled Jesse off stable duty and put him in the dining room, where more than a hundred people wanted tea, coffee, snacks and ideas for the wedding decorations. Jesse went from pouring tea to stringing little white lights from ceiling to wall to floor.

Timmy took exception to all the people and hid under a table near the edge of the dining room. No one seemed to mind, and two motherly types provided him with paper and pens. Eva followed the bride around, clipboard in hand, taking notes furiously and offering suggestions that the bride didn't seem overly inclined to take.

"We've already made the punch," Eva said. "It's too late to change the flavor."

"But I found this awesome recipe for cherry punch and—"

Jesse had to give Eva credit. Within ten minutes,

the bride was paying for a second punch offering instead of replacing the first one.

Yup, Eva was good at business.

Jacob sat in the dining room with the groom's father, who looked a bit shell-shocked. Jesse overheard him say that he and his wife had eloped.

It was after eleven before Jesse and Timmy checked on the horses and then climbed the stairs to the apartment. To Jesse's surprise, Timmy went to the fridge and poured himself a glass of milk and got a handful of cookies.

"Put them on a plate," Jesse directed him. So far, Timmy hadn't embraced Jesse's need to keep the apartment clean. The little boy was willing to leave food sitting on the table for days.

Timmy got a plate and sat at the table.

"Not tired?" Jesse asked next.

Timmy shook his head.

"Me either." First thing Jesse did was get his own plate of cookies and some milk. Then he took some paper and pencils from the drawer next to the sink. Sitting across from his son, he checked tomorrow's schedule. There was something planned for every minute.

It was time to follow Elise's advice.

"Okay, Timmy, from now on, we're going to keep track of our daily activities."

Jesse wrote a number one on his paper. Out loud, he stated, "We can start with the past. One, Monday I filled out a declaration of paternity with the Arizona Office of Vital Records." Leaning closer to Timmy, he said, "That means I'm telling the government that I'm your dad."

For once, Timmy didn't look at his hands. He stared at Jesse, though still with no expression.

"Two, Wednesday I led a group on a trail ride all by myself."

Timmy hadn't picked up his pencil, and he stared at the piece of paper as if it would bite him. Finally Jesse figured it out. He switched the notebook paper for typewriter paper and drew a line straight down and straight across.

"You can draw something you accomplished."

Timmy nodded, rose from the chair and went over to fetch his crayons from inside the makeshift fort.

If Jesse ever were to go to court, he'd need evidence that he tried to be a good father, tried to do what the state required. Even if his paper trail was homemade and half of it done with crayons, he'd have one.

"Three, yesterday I attended my first anger management class. Though I'm not sure why I need to do this. Anger is not one of my vices, never has been."

During his life, Jesse had learned that holding back a few steps, letting a situation lose steam before he reacted, often saved both time and energy.

It also saved lives.

"Not on my list, but something you should know," Jesse continued, "is I made an appointment with a child psychologist. That's someone whose goal will be helping you with your problems. Both the lawyer and my probation officer made phone calls, and we got you an appointment come Monday."

Timmy paid no attention, but he did follow Jesse's directions. He was drawing accomplishments. In the top box, a black-and-white pony appeared with a small boy riding him.

"That's a good choice," Jesse complimented him. "Four," Jesse said, "I had my first request for a private lesson. Granted, the client knows more than I do about horses, but still, it's a start."

Crystal didn't scare off easily. She'd arrived for her second lesson yesterday and did pretty much the same thing as she'd done on Tuesday. She'd mentioned her single status three times, talked about a great movie showing downtown that she hadn't seen yet and went out of her way to be nice to Timmy.

"Some kids," she'd said knowingly, "talk late because everyone else does the talking for them."

Jesse guessed Crystal was too busy talking to notice that *he* didn't do much talking, either. It did make him wonder, though, who in Timmy's past might have done all the talking.

Thinking about that lesson spurred him to ask Timmy, "Did you notice Jacob and Eva watching us?"

Timmy stopped working on the pony he was drawing in the second box. Putting his crayon down, he stood, walked over to the window and looked toward the main house.

"Yeah," Jesse said softly. "I wonder what she's doing, too."

While his son stood at the window, Jesse pulled the Bible from on top of the refrigerator and turned to the second chapter of Genesis. Last night, he'd decided to start reading the Bible aloud every night, chapter by chapter, to Timmy.

As he read, Jesse realized he didn't need to keep a written record of glorifying God. The Bible, praying—they weren't goals, they weren't successes anymore, they were as much a part of him as eating and breathing.

He had a new goal, though. He was going to help Eva get over her fear of horses.

Brittney Hope Reese wasn't a bridezilla. No, she was more a control freak who was out of control. What she should have done was hire a wedding planner. Instead, she chose to do it herself, and every time a better idea occurred to her, she wanted to do away with the old one.

Which was okay if she was doing away with

ideas she'd spent her own money on. Saturday, the day of the wedding, she was trying to spend Eva's money.

"I'm sorry I forgot to call you about the color change," Brittney said. "Is there any way we can switch out the flowers on the tables? I'd really prefer blue."

The tables were already half set up with off-white tablecloths. The centerpieces were candles and pink flowers. Under the table closest to the door connecting the lobby to the dining room, Timmy played with a small truck. He'd taken some of the extra pink flowers and made a road.

Instead of rolling her eyes, Eva looked at her notebook. "Did you bring blue flowers?"

"No, I was hoping you might have some in storage?"

"Everything we have in storage has to do with running a ranch, not running a wedding."

For a moment, Eva thought Brittney was going to argue, not that there was anything to argue about. Then Brittney's soon-to-be husband called her over, and all was forgotten.

The dining room was turning into a wedding wonderland, and Eva had to admit, Brittney had taste.

And money.

Pity she didn't have the organization skills to put the combination to optimal use. But if she wasn't perfectly happy with the finished product, then she had no one but herself to blame. Some things simply couldn't be changed at the last minute.

Eva headed across the room, where Patti was working on a trellis that would arch across the kitchen door. Brittney wanted every part of the dining room to look wedding-ready.

"I don't know how to get it so that when the door swings open, the trellis doesn't go flying," Patti complained. "Twice Cook's come out and about knocked it over. My back's killing me. I never dreamed this would take so long."

"I'll finish it," Eva offered. "You go back to the lobby and manage the phones and desk."

The trellis was made out of white chicken wire. Brittney or somebody had decorated it with gauze and tiny red flowers. It was simple and didn't weigh enough to stay upright should a person sneeze.

Pushing it flush against the wall, Eva looked for something she could attach it to. Brittney—make that her father—had brought along plenty of twist ties, but Eva wasn't sure how to fasten them. Nothing jutted from the walls. No errant nails waited.

She arranged the trellis so the saloon doors where the kitchen staff exited and entered were centered. Maybe she needed to get some cement blocks and try to hold it steady via a foundation. A little duct tape might help, too.

Cook came out the door, bumping against the

trellis and sending it crashing into Eva. Eva made to steady it, but it fell on top of her awkwardly, trapping her. Cook simply looked at her, smiling, and said, "You've got to be kidding."

Two strong arms came around her neck, lifting the trellis up and holding it steady. She didn't need to turn around to know whose arms were rescuing her. And they certainly didn't belong to Cook.

Jesse Campbell.

"Kind of a silly thing," he said. His chin was right above her head, so close she could have nestled in had she wanted.

She wanted.

Instead she said, "And the silly thing needs to be secured here so that it doesn't fall over every time Cook opens the door."

It took Jesse a few seconds to stand it back up. When he did, and his arms went from around her to around the trellis, Eva definitely felt a sense of loss.

She resolutely pushed the feeling aside.

He was an ex-con with a kid and carried so much baggage he almost needed his own luggage cart.

"What exactly are you trying to do?" he asked.

She told him. In just ten minutes, he found some nails plus a hammer. By simply twisting the chicken wire around the nail heads and hammering the nails into the wall, he was able to secure the trellis.

She added yet one more skill to his growing list. He could ride, he could cook and he could fix things.

"Did you learn how to fix things in prison, too?"

He smiled, but this time he didn't look annoyed at her question. "Most of it I learned on my own when I was growing up. I practically raised myself. When something broke, I fixed it. But to answer your question, I learned woodworking and took an upholstery class while incarcerated."

He picked up a flower that had dropped to the ground. Instead of returning it to the trellis, he stuck it in her hair, right above her ear.

"I can use a sewing machine now," he bragged. "That's something I didn't know before going in. But I'll never be in your league, with that loom."

"You know," Eva said, "in the Hopi culture, it's usually the men who do the weaving."

"Really? Why?"

"A hundred years ago, the women had too much to do every day. It was the men who had the time."

"Well, I had a lot of time in prison. I'm actually a pretty good upholsterer. Course, in prison, minimum wage is eighty cents."

It was the dose of reality she'd needed. He'd been in prison. For five years.

"Were you really guilty?" she whispered.

He let go of the trellis, tugging at it a little as if

checking its reliability. He didn't need to check. She knew he'd secured it.

"Your dad didn't tell you?"

"Just that you'd paid your dues."

He handed her the hammer and the extra five nails. Then he took a step back. "I was really guilty. You'd be wise to keep that in mind."

She'd spoiled the mood, and she didn't know if she was annoyed at herself or relieved.

His steps were purposeful as he walked away. Gone was the easy manner she'd come to expect.

He'd almost made it to the back door when a blonde woman entered the room from the lobby. For a moment, the woman looked confused. Then she cupped her hands around her mouth and said loudly, "I'm looking for Timmy or Jesse Campbell."

Eva saw two things. First, Timmy crawled farther under the table. Second, Jesse pivoted, assessed the woman and frowned as he walked her way.

"I'm Jesse."

"Good," the woman said, more to herself than to Jesse. Looking around, she asked, "And where is your son? Where is Timmy?"

Like a piece of steel drawn to a magnet, Eva headed over. She didn't know this woman, and it looked like Jesse didn't either.

Eva watched as Jesse's back straightened, and he

raised himself to his full height. Something about this woman had his dander up. Eva's, too.

"I don't believe we've been introduced," he said. "Are you part of the wedding?"

The woman blinked, looked around and then gave a halfhearted smile. "No." She pulled a card from her shirt pocket and handed it to Jesse.

Eva couldn't get to his side fast enough. "I'm Eva Hubrecht. This is my ranch. May I help you?"

"You employ Mr. Campbell?" the woman asked.

"I do."

Jesse, looking shocked, handed Eva the card. She glanced at it, taking in every word. Rene Comstocker, Child Protective Services.

"I'm investigating a complaint we received yesterday about possible neglect. Mr. Campbell, I'd like to talk with Timmy. Where is he?"

Both Jesse and Eva looked at the table directly to their left. The social worker frowned and then raised the tablecloth. Underneath, eyes closed and visibly shaking, Timmy was curled in a fetal position with his thumb in his mouth.

Chapter Thirteen

Jesse felt the anger start to rise to the top. For once, holding it in might not work. He'd been doing exactly what the law told him to do! He was staying out of trouble, meeting with his parole officer and attending anger management classes as scheduled, all while learning to be and fighting to be a parent to a special-needs child.

And now this!

His eyes narrowed, and he tried not to let the frustration, the sheer fury, come out with his words.

"You will not—" he began.

Eva's hand on his arm was the only thing that kept him from finishing with "—touch my son."

"Ms. Comstocker," Eva broke in, "let's meet in my office for a few moments. Timmy's fine under the table."

"I'd rather talk with Timmy first." Ms. Comstocker squatted down, holding a corner of the tablecloth in the air. “Hey, how you doing down there, little guy? Are you all right?”

Jesse stepped forward, unable and unwilling to listen to Eva. He’d drag Ms. Comstocker away from Timmy if he had to. There’d been four days with no fetal position. And the thumb sucking would never go away if people kept interfering. First the police officer who thought Jesse stole a car. And now this woman who thought Jesse would neglect his child.

Neglect his child!

“Trust me,” Eva whispered to him.

Jesse was getting tired of trusting people. So far, it seemed, trust was getting him nowhere. “He’s going to start crying in a minute. Last time it took—”

“Please,” Eva added. “Elise talks about this all the time. I know what to do.”

Something about the words, the look in Eva’s eyes, the compassion, got through just in time. Jesse tried to relax, tried to unclench his teeth and let go of the fists he’d formed.

Be assertive, not aggressive. Lesson one from the single anger management class he’d attended. Curtly he nodded to Eva, giving her the go-ahead.

Turning to Ms. Comstocker, she said, “Timmy’s mute. He’s not going to speak with you, and you’re scaring him.”

Ms. Comstocker remained in a squat for a few minutes. Then she looked around. Most of the people in the room had stopped decorating. They were watching her.

"Just come to my office," Eva urged her. "We can talk, answer your questions there. We fully intend to comply with you."

"I'd rather stay where I can see the boy."

"As you can see," Eva pointed out, "we're getting ready for a wedding. This room will be chaotic for the rest of the day—certainly not suitable for a serious conversation. Timmy was under the table when you arrived. It's safe to leave him there. Look, there's his toy truck, and you can see he's made a road out of the flowers. He's been playing under the table for more than an hour. He's in the fetal position and sucking his thumb because you're a stranger scaring him."

Ms. Comstocker looked from Timmy to the door to the crowd in the room.

To Jesse's surprise, it was Brittney, the bride, who joined in the conversation. "She's telling the truth. It's my wedding tonight, so I've been in here all day. The little boy came in this morning and ate breakfast. Once my family and friends came in to start decorating, he scooted under the table to play with his truck, and he's been there ever since. Hasn't said a word."

"I gave him a stick of gum," a matronly woman added. "Now I know why he didn't thank me."

Jesse battled the piece of him that wanted to explode. On the one hand—wow, people were actually speaking up in his defense. Strangers even. On the other—once again, Jesse's past, his current situation, were all on display for the world to see.

"If my office won't do," Eva continued, "we can sit on the couch by the front desk. We'll prop this door open so the table is in full sight. Look, I'll pull the tablecloth up so you can see him."

Ms. Comstocker finally nodded.

Okay, maybe letting Eva do this the calm way had worked. But the meeting wasn't over yet. Jesse followed Ms. Comstocker and Eva through door, which he propped open. Behind him, Timmy immediately began keening. Ms. Comstocker turned, eyes assessing.

Jesse went back, got down on his knees, and said, "This one's easy. I won't be leaving. I'll be sitting on the couch. You can see me. All Ms. Comstocker's going to do is ask questions. That's all. And I know you were listening. If you want to help, get out from under the table and come sit beside me while she asks questions."

Blank look.

For almost two weeks, Jesse'd been befuddled by the blank look. Now it just made him want to cry.

He joined the two women again. He sat next to Eva—who was on her cell phone, apparently talking with her sister—and looked at Ms. Comstocker. Timmy stopped keening, She cleared her throat. "We received a call that you often punish your son by locking him in closets or forcing him under tables and denying him food."

"I—"

Eva's hand went on his leg. Nope, he wasn't letting her dictate this meeting. She wasn't a parent.

A parent.

He was a parent.

"My son's gained five pounds in the two weeks I've had him. I've never locked him in a closet. The closet in my apartment doesn't even have a lock. He eats his meals in here, as plenty of people have seen." The anger still wanted to explode, still wanted to take over the meeting.

But something else fought to the surface. A tiny rational thought reminded him that he had a dozen witnesses to how Timmy had been treated these past two weeks.

"As for neglect—" Jesse began.

Timmy walked into the room, which went silent—even Eva stopped her phone conversation—and Jesse noticed something he'd started to take for granted. His son was clean. His clothes were, too. His hair was combed. He'd mimicked Jesse this morning. His teeth were brushed. Same mimicking. And there wasn't a single bruise or scratch on him.

That had never been the case when a child protective agent showed up back when Jesse was a kid.

How could he have forgotten?

Maybe because the two times it happened, his mother had been belligerent. Both times, Jesse'd been removed from the home for safety reasons. Not that the relatives he'd wound up staying with had provided a safer environment.

For a five-year-old, Timmy knew how to give a dirty look. It was an expression Jesse had never before seen on his child's face, and he hoped he never had to see it again. Five-year-olds should be worrying whether Scooby-Doo will solve the mystery and what flavor ice cream to order next time. They shouldn't be worrying about what the child protection officer might do.

"Hi, Timmy," Ms. Comstocker said, ignoring the look. "I'm glad you joined us."

Timmy sat next to Jesse. An inch closer and he'd be in Jesse's lap. Timmy put his hand on Jesse's knee.

Okay, so the kid's fingernails were dirty.

"You've had custody for two weeks?" Ms. Comstocker asked.

"I've had him for almost two weeks," Jesse answered, avoiding the word custody.

"You like living with your father?" Ms. Comstocker asked. "How does he treat you?"

Eva ended her phone call, but Jesse didn't need her help as he cautioned, "You'll have to settle for one yes-or-no question at a time."

Ms. Comstocker nodded. "Timmy, do you and your father get along?"

Timmy nodded.

Eva joined the conversation. "Jesse, Elise says to answer all her questions. She says to contact your lawyer as soon as possible. And she says to take pictures of Timmy as he looks right now, with Ms. Comstocker. I can do that." She pulled her cell phone from her pocket and immediately snapped two.

"Who's Elise?" Ms. Comstocker asked.

"Elise is my sister. She's a social worker in Two Mules, Arizona. I called her to find out exactly what we should do."

Ms. Comstocker pursed her lips. "Mr. Campbell should answer my questions. That's what he should do."

"Ask away," Jesse said.

Ms. Comstocker didn't ask Jesse, though. Instead, she turned to Timmy. "Has your father ever put you someplace you weren't happy, where you were scared, a dark someplace?"

Jesse interrupted. "He came to me scared. That's an unfair question."

Ms. Comstocker looked away from Timmy and right at Jesse. "What do you mean?"

Jesse pulled out his wallet. "Here, take these phone numbers. The first one is for my parole officer. The second one is for my child custody lawyer. If you'd waited a week, I'd have a number for the child psychologist Timmy and I will be seeing come Monday."

"My, you've been busy for only two weeks." Ms. Comstocker took the cards Jesse offered and typed the information on some electronic gadget Jesse hadn't even noticed she'd been carrying.

"What Jesse's trying to tell you," Eva said, her voice soothing, "is that until two weeks ago, he didn't even know he had a son."

"The boy's mother didn't tell you?" Ms. Comstocker asked.

"No, she didn't tell me."

"How did he come to live with you?"

Once more, Jesse told the abbreviated version. He knew from the expression on the child custody officer's face that she wasn't liking anything he was saying.

"You're certain you are the boy's father?" was the first question out of her mouth when he finished talking.

Jesse looked at Timmy instead of Ms. Comstocker. "Yes, I'm Timmy's father."

It took a half hour, a tour of Jesse's upstairs

apartment, and a phone call to the senior Kildare of Kildare and Sons to satisfy Ms. Rene Comstocker that Timmy's needs were being met and that his ventures under tables and sleeping in a makeshift fort were his way of removing himself from situations rather than Jesse's way of punishing him.

Meeting Pinocchio the pony was the only time she smiled.

When Ms. Comstocker finally gathered her purse and briefcase, she made it clear that she wasn't leaving for good. "While I believe that Timmy's forays under the table are not an issue you're responsible for, Timmy is still a child in need. Today was just the start of an initial assessment, and I have many concerns."

"Will this hurt my chances of getting legal guardianship?" Jesse's voice cracked. He hated showing weakness. He hated that he was trying to do the right thing, the right way, and for every step forward there were two steps back.

"That will depend on my final analysis after I feel I've gotten all the information. I'll be making more inquiries," Ms. Comstocker promised. "And I'll be looking for a way to speak, er, communicate with Timmy privately. I need to get a clear picture of what's going on here, because quite honestly, I've never had so many unanswered questions and loose ends."

Jesse and Eva followed her out to her car.

"Next time, I'll probably bring a police officer with me, just in case."

"You won't need a police officer," Eva said. "You won't find any reason to doubt that Jesse's a good dad."

It was just what Jesse needed to hear.

Jesse strode off, Timmy stumbling behind. Before Eva had time to make a real decision about what to do next—follow them or leave them alone—the back door of the dining hall opened. Patti called out, "I need you!"

Patti had been handling the front desk and helping Cook, all because Eva wasn't around to do front desk duty and Jesse was supposed to be doing kitchen duty.

"We've got to find someone to help Cook and fast," Eva decided.

"Jesse not going to be able to help?"

"I don't know, and I'm not going to ask."

It was her father who finally saved the day. He, his rodeo buddy and his buddy's wife all headed for the kitchen. Eva didn't like the look on her father's face. He looked drawn, tired and dismayed.

Not his usual look.

But then, he truly hated anything to do with the kitchen.

She didn't have the chance to question her dad about where he'd been while the child protective officer was at the ranch, because the phone never stopped ringing, the bride never ran out of new ideas and the frequent trips to the back porch to scope out the property took up all her time.

She saw Jesse and Timmy only once. They were on horseback, taking off up one of the trails. What was he thinking? It was a hundred and seven in the shade!

She knew the answer. He was thinking too much and wanted the ride to clear his head. She hoped he came to the right conclusion and soon. She went hunting for her father and found him doing dishes. His shirt was damp and stuck to his back. His cowboy hat was propped on the edge of a baker's rack. His hair was plastered to his face. Not his best look.

"Dad, did you hear about—"

"Yes, I've had at least two guests and Mitch tell me what was going on."

"I need Mike Hamm's number."

Her dad shut the door on the commercial dishwasher and frowned at her. "Why?"

"I think Mike needs to come out here today. Jesse needs him."

"If Jesse needs him, then Jesse can call him."

"You weren't around when the child protection officer showed up. You didn't see how upset he was."

"I see how upset you are," her father pointed out. "And I'm not sure why. You didn't want him here in the first place. You told me we couldn't afford him. I'm starting to think you were right."

Eva paused. They couldn't afford Jesse, but it seemed such an irrelevant point right now. "No, I wasn't right. He's doing great. You were right when you said everyone deserves a second chance."

Her father turned back to the dishwasher and picked up a tray of glasses that had just cooled down. "You need to stay out of it. I'm starting to question whether or not Jesse belongs here."

This was not what she expected. Not at all.

"I need more plates," Cook shouted, and her dad turned away. End of discussion.

Eva didn't care how busy she was. She marched to the front desk, turned on the computer and looked Mike up online. Since he was a minister, he wasn't that hard to find.

She had him on the phone a minute later.

"Eva Hubrecht," he said. "I've been trying to get over your way. I've even talked to the wife about making a day of it, bringing the baby."

"Baby?"

"Didn't Jesse tell you? My wife gave birth right before Jesse's release. Otherwise I'd have picked him up and delivered him to your doorstep."

And Jesse hadn't complained, Eva thought, not even when the alternative wound up being his mother.

"I'd love to see you," Mike continued, "and hear

how you feel Jesse's doing. He's really taking on a lot."

"Has he called you?"

"Once or twice. Sure is bad luck that he wound up with a stolen car."

"Mike, can you come today? Please. Jesse needs you."

"Why? What's happened now?"

Quickly Eva filled him in on the day's events. When she finished, he was silent for a moment. "Eva, why is it that you're calling me instead of your father?"

"I think Dad's getting exasperated. But I'm not. You should see the good Jesse's doing, not just working here but especially with Timmy."

"Eva," Mike said, "there's not one thing that I can do that you can't. And I'm thinking you might do a better job than me."

"What?"

"You've obviously built a rapport with both Jesse and Timmy. I haven't met Timmy yet. And you're the one sitting there helping Jesse out with everything that has happened so far. Given your sister's job, you have good advice. Don't give up on Jesse. That young man will surprise you."

More likely, that young man would be the death of her. He was one emotional catastrophe after another.

"I won't," she sputtered, thinking this was more

than she'd bargained for. A little outside help would be appreciated.

"Let's say a prayer before we hang up," Mike suggested.

"Jesse needs a whole lot more than prayer," she retorted.

"Oh, I think the Lord knows just what Jesse needs." Mike started in on a prayer before Eva could say anything else.

Hanging up after the amen, Eva knew one thing. She felt better. She just wished Jesse could have been part of the prayer.

Heading back to the dining room, she was in time to watch as chaos turned to perfection and the bride and groom walked, arm in arm, through the door. It all came together. Eva was amazed. She put the phone on answering machine so that she and Patti—and even a couple of the guests—could help serve. Eva worked the salad stand. If anyone could tell her mind wasn't on ranch dressing, they were polite enough not to mention it. Looking around, she tried to find Jesse or her father.

Neither made an appearance.

Checking her watch, she felt a flutter of concern. She understood Jesse's need to get away, understood that work was the last thing Jesse wanted to deal with right now. He needed time with his son. But he was scheduled to take the bride and groom on an evening ride after the meal was finished and as the sun started to set. Brittney wanted pictures with the horses and the sunset both before the vows and after.

There were a couple of toasts, and then Brittney announced, "There's an hour and a half before we actually have the ceremony. There'll be a dance in here afterward, and that's when we'll have the cake. Thank you all." She teared up. "This is the best night of my life."

People started moving. The help cleaned. The guests headed for the doors, probably thinking they'd have time for a quick dip in the pool or a nap before the ceremony. Brittney headed for Eva. "It's time to get ready for our ride."

Where was Jesse? They needed him to lead this ride. Her father couldn't do it. His toe was hurting more than he let on. Mitch would do it, but he had a tendency to hurry things along, which was not what Brittney wanted tonight.

"I've got the horses saddled and ready. They're just outside the door."

Eva let out a breath she hadn't realized she was holding.

Jesse, his lips in a thin line, stood behind her. Timmy was at his side. Both were sweaty, covered with a thin layer of dust—and to her eyes, they had never looked better.

"You sure?" she asked.

"I'm sure."

By the time Brittney and her groom walked out the back door, picture perfect in new Western clothes, Jesse was pretending to smile.

No one else probably realized that he was pretending.

Because no one else, at least here in Apache Creek, Arizona, knew him quite as well as Eva did. Not even Mike Hamm.

Later, when the last kiss had been shared, publicly, and the last cake crumb wiped from a table, Eva collapsed in the back of the room and said, "Remind me next time someone wants to have a wedding that I'm not a wedding planner."

Patti chuckled. "You did a good job. Your daddy's proud."

At least as proud as he could be about her keeping the lodging part of their ranch—the part he didn't care about—successful.

"I'm so tired I didn't even look," Eva confessed. "What do we have on the agenda for tomorrow?"

"We're full, but it's a typical day. Most of the guests are staying on. We have both horseback and bicycle rides reserved."

"On a Sunday? Did my dad authorize that?"

"I guess the bride's father told your father that if he'd arrange a breakfast ride, most of the riders would be willing to attend church afterward."

Eva's mouth opened. "That's bribery."

Patti grinned. “And it worked. Well, I’m out of here.”

After saying good-night to Cook, who was still doing some prep for breakfast, Eva headed for her rooms, changed into comfortable clothes, and then went to the living room. She was tired but also wired, and probably too worried about what was going on with Jesse Campbell even to think about sleep yet. She needed to clear her mind. Settling down in front of her loom, she took a strand of brown wool and began weaving and working the shuttle stick, something she could usually do with her eyes closed. Tonight, though, she had to concentrate. This blanket was about two-thirds finished. It didn’t have a buyer. Finally, after a good half hour, she stopped. Her work wasn’t up to her usual standard. She sat back and looked at what she’d accomplished. She’d been a little heavy-handed. Her weaving was tight, angry.

Like she was.

“Ahem.” Her father stood in the doorway, looking at her, still as drawn and tired-looking as this morning.

“Where have you been?” Eva asked.

“Out in the barn, talking with Jesse.”

“Dad, you can’t be upset with Jesse,” Eva burst out. “This isn’t his fault.”

“I told him when I hired him that I had misgivings. He promised me there’d be no problems. In the past two weeks, there have been lots of problems. I'm beginning to regret giving in."

"You'd be bored if there were no problems," Eva argued. "You've always loved a challenge."

"I was younger then. Now I've got a ranch that's making more money because of a wedding than because of the horses, and I've got a broken toe, and I'm starting to wonder if the drunk who ran it over was here to meet up with Jesse."

"Dad, whatever gave you that idea? Jesse didn't know him!"

"How do you know?"

"He'd have said something."

"Depends on what they were planning."

"Dad, when has Jesse had time to plan anything? He's been busy day and night. I know with my heart that the drunk wasn't here to meet up with Jesse."

"How do you know that? Little girl, you've known him two weeks and you're way too trusting. That concerns me."

"I—"

"Conversation over. I think I'll give him the name of a friend of mine in Utah. Perhaps it's best he relocate."

"Relocate! He can't. It would be a violation of his parole. And even if he got approval, he's trying to get custody. If he leaves the state, he'll have to start over."

"Sometimes starting over is the best thing."

"But, Dad, he—" Eva stood, turning to face her father, completely dumbfounded. This was not the way Jacob Hubrecht dealt with people. He'd always followed the creed "Innocent until proven guilty." It was the cowboy way, he said.

"You've got this ranch to take care of," Jacob said. "Don't be adding any more to your plate. Especially not someone who's made one poor decision after another and who's going to be moving on soon." He turned and walked away.

Eva knew if she said anything else, especially if she emphasized that Jesse hadn't made any poor decisions since he'd gotten here, she'd be responsible for changing the moving on from "soon" to "now."

She also knew that somebody'd been talking to her dad, saying that Jesse was more trouble than he was worth.

Who?

And why did her dad believe it?

The question bothered her clear into the next day, Sunday, when Eva stayed busy answering questions and giving directions to their full house of guests. True to their word, a good number of the wedding party were heading to church as payment for the breakfast ride.

Jesse and Timmy were in the dining hall. Jesse was teaching his son the fine art of dicing potatoes.

"Is it safe to let him use a knife?" Eva asked. "What if Ms. Comstocker shows up?"

"Can't second-guess everything," Jesse said. "Timmy needs to have some life skills, and so far, cooking is an area he's pretty good at. He can even crack eggs."

Timmy smiled but didn't meet Eva's eyes.

"I heard my dad talked to you last night. So, are you thinking about heading for Utah?"

"I can't see it happening soon," Jesse said.

Now *he* wasn't meeting Eva's eyes.

"Dad doesn't mean it. Something happened yesterday, and I'm not sure what. He wasn't around all morning, and he should have been."

She didn't have long to dwell on it. Someone called Eva's name, and next thing she knew, she was climbing in the passenger side of one of the Lost Dutchman trucks. Two guests were in the back. She started to ask her dad how Jesse and Timmy were getting to church but thought better of it.

"You guys put on a great wedding," the woman sitting behind Eva said. "I thought July would make a horrible date, but you managed to pull it off."

"The bride had all the ideas. She's the one who turned the programs into fans and who put water bottles on all the chairs."

Brittney'd also paid someone to remove the

water bottle labels and replace them with a strip that contained photos of herself and the groom and the date of their wedding.

"Still," the woman continued, "I watched you scurrying around."

"Eva's got a degree in marketing. She's taking the Lost Dutchman ranch to a new level," Jacob said.

Eva was surprised. Her dad never bragged on her. He'd always downplayed the lodging part of the Lost Dutchman.

"Everything okay with the man and his son? I felt so sorry for him."

Jacob answered before Eva could. "Everything's fine. No need to worry."

When they got to church, Eva finally found Jesse and Timmy. They'd ridden with Harold. He'd also carted another family with them.

Their little church would be full.

She caught sight of Jesse only once or twice as Bible class ended and the service began. After the final amen sounded and all the goodbyes were said, Eva followed her dad out the door. Down the far end of the parking lot, Harold held open the door of his truck for the guests he'd driven. Then he hopped in himself and drove down the road.

Jesse and Timmy were supposed to be with him.

They weren't.

Chapter Fourteen

Harold only shrugged when Jesse announced he had plans and didn't need a ride back to the Lost Dutchman.

In truth, Jesse's only plan was to figure out what to do next, and he needed to be away from the ranch to do that.

The morning church service, about Paul's spiritual journey, had been hard for Jesse to hear, and he wasn't sure he completely understood. Paul had been born to wealth—had been educated and probably had been loved. Jesse had been born to chaos, had dropped out of school in the tenth grade and had never felt loved.

But God had come looking for him just as he'd gone looking for Paul, just not so dramatically.

Paul had done prison time, a little more than five years just like Jesse, yet he'd done time because he'd been preaching the word, doing something right for society. Jesse's prison time was for something he'd done wrong, so wrong, and no matter how Jesse had tried to atone for his sins, they were still on his conscience.

One more difference was that Paul was arrested and incarcerated four times, if Jesse understood the preacher. Jesse only once.

So far.

Those words kept popping up whenever Jesse thought about his future. Despite the prediction from the guard, he hadn't been sent back to prison yet. But how long would that remain true? He couldn't shake the memories of the stolen car and now the child protective officer. Why were these things happening? What was he doing wrong?

Looking down at Timmy standing by his side, he wondered if he was being fair to the boy. Maybe there was a home somewhere for Timmy, with two parents who'd love him. He knew there were awesome foster families out there. The kid certainly didn't deserve a mother who'd just drop him off or a father who was fresh out of prison and stumbling all over himself just trying to survive. Jesse wanted so badly to be a good father to him—but maybe doing what was best for Timmy meant letting him go.

"Let's get something to eat," Jesse finally said. He didn't want to go back to the Lost Dutchman. Yet even though every fiber of his being said *run*, he didn't know where to go. And with a five-year-old, his choices were limited. But the biggest hindrance was knowing that if he ran, he'd lose everything.

And yet if he stayed, he might lose everything anyway.

He wasn't a gambling man, but he didn't need to be to figure his odds sounded like maybe lose or definitely lose.

Was it even possible to win?

Timmy followed Jesse, uncomplaining and sometimes doing a little half run to keep up as the hot Arizona sun slow-roasted them. By the time they made it to the Miner's Lamp only two blocks from the church, both were thirsty, sweaty and wiped out.

The Miner's Lamp clearly catered to the church crowd. Jesse recognized a few of the faces from church. They'd wisely driven the two blocks so they didn't have bright red faces.

"Hey, good to see you!" Jane de la Rosa came up, grabbed two menus and motioned for Jesse to follow her. She led them to a booth. She handed Timmy the child's menu and a few crayons and asked what they wanted to drink.

"I'll have iced tea, and Timmy can have a Sprite."

Timmy's eyes opened wide. At the ranch, he was only allowed milk, water and an occasional orange juice. Every time he reached for a soda, Jesse took it away from him.

Because Jesse'd seen Eva do that the very first morning.

"Sometimes," Jesse told him now, "we have to celebrate even when there seems to be nothing to celebrate."

Timmy nodded and started coloring. Already Jesse could see that horses were, once again, his first choice.

After figuring out what he wanted to order, Jesse pulled out his wallet and studied the business cards filling the slots where there should be library cards, credit cards, maybe even AAA. Instead he had a driver's license and all these cards. He had his lawyer's, his parole officer's and now the child protective officer's. Tomorrow he'd have the child psychologist's.

He also had one for the Lost Dutchman ranch. The main number was on the front. On the blank back, Jesse had scribbled both Jacob's and Eva's private cell phone numbers.

He'd never called Eva's. He'd called Jacob a time or two, always about ranch stuff.

Jane returned with their drinks, took their order and disappeared.

Jesse pushed his wallet aside and studied his son. He had no doubt that Timmy was his. None.

"Timmy," Jesse said, leaning forward, "are you happy living with me?"

Timmy nodded.

"Are you happy living at the Lost Dutchman?"

Again Timmy nodded, this time a bit more vigorously.

"We might not get to stay," Jesse said.

Blank look.

Jesse slid the business cards in front of Timmy and told him what each one meant. "These people are helping us—but there's a chance they might also try to separate us. I'm thinking we're in this together. And we should stay together, even if we have to leave here, right?"

Blank look.

"You are happy living with me?"

A nod.

"If we need to leave, will you come with me?"

Blank look.

For a moment, Jesse felt exasperation. Then, as Jane set their meal in front of them, he settled back. It finally occurred to him that Jesse's blank look was an answer—it just happened to be an answer that didn't fall under the yes/no category. It was "I can't deal with this."

"You want to stay here?"

A nod. Timmy made no move to touch his food.

"Okay, Timmy, we'll stay here and fight. But you'll need to help, just like yesterday when you came and sat down next to me when Ms. Comstocker was asking questions. Can you do that?"

Timmy nodded.

Jesse picked up his hamburger and took a bite, all the while studying his son. In two weeks, the time Jesse had had him, Timmy had gained weight, taken more than a dozen hose showers and almost stopped sucking his thumb.

All positives.

As if to prove Jesse had made the right decision by choosing to stay and fight, Timmy picked up a chicken finger with one hand and continued drawing with the other.

One by one, Jesse picked up the business cards described what they were, and asked, "Did your mother take you to any of these places?"

Timmy shook his head at the lawyer, the pediatrician and the child psychologist. He nodded at Child Protective Services.

"Here in Arizona?" Jesse asked.

Timmy shook his head.

"Where?"

Timmy shrugged.

"Did she need to?"

Blank look.

Jesse let the conversation go. Tomorrow, when they met the child psychologist, he'd share the conversation and maybe get some answers.

In the meantime, Jesse studied the card belonging to the Lost Dutchman Ranch and turned it over. Eva Hubrecht had written her name in tight, looping cursive.

If he took a moment to listen to his heart, he'd accept that part of him wanted to stay because of her. But allowing Eva into his heart would only lead to heartbreak.

It was almost eight when he made it back to the Lost Dutchman. He wasn't quite willing to think of it as home. Jane pulled in front of the main house. Timmy had the back door open and was out before Jesse managed to undo his seat belt. His son wanted to see Pinocchio.

"Thanks." Jesse was a little embarrassed that he'd had to accept a ride from the friendly waitress, but Jane had insisted. She was definitely her mother's daughter. Both Patti and Jane were gregarious, outspoken and funny.

Eva was reserved, outspoken and funny. She was more a mystery than an open book.

Walking into the lobby, Jesse knew who he needed to see, but he doubted he'd be welcomed by Jacob Hubrecht as enthusiastically as Timmy would be by Pinocchio.

A sign on the desk said Ring for Service.

Was it just last week he'd felt welcome enough to knock on the left side door and walk back to the family's living area?

The thought made him want to turn away. However, with all that he was dealing with, he could use some direction. And since his whole life—besides church—was here at the Lost Dutchman, he needed to find his direction here.

From behind the left side door, he could hear country music playing.

Eva.

His hand didn't press down on the bell. His mind wouldn't issue the order.

Turning, he went through the door on the right and entered the dining hall. There was a family in the game room. Mom, dad, two kids. When one shouted "UNO!" he knew what they were doing. Being a family.

Staying a family was one of his goals. Getting to the point where he didn't have to work at it—where he and Timmy could just *be* a family—seemed a distant dream.

Tea and water were available. The door to the kitchen was open to a sterile room. Without Cook, it was empty. One man made a powerful difference. Cook for the kitchen. Harold for the stables; Eva for the main house.

Jesus, for them all.

Pouring himself a glass of tea, Jesse sat at one of the corner tables and tried to rid his mind of all the clutter. He was exhausted. And he feared what lay ahead would be even worse. In his case, it looked like he wasn't a man who could make a powerful difference. Not if he lost Timmy.

Leaning back, he closed his eyes. He didn't want to go back to the little apartment, where a fort took up half the living room and crayon-scrawled pictures covered the refrigerator and—

"Jesse." Her voice, her scent, her power.

"I was looking for a little alone time." Mumbling seemed the best response.

"Then why are you in the dining hall?"

He wanted to laugh. She had a point. No other room was as utilized on the Lost Dutchman as this room. He couldn't do anything right. He couldn't even manage to find alone time on a ranch that covered four hundred sixty-two acres.

"How did you get back home? And where have you been? You were gone for hours."

"You miss me?" He opened his eyes, sat up and stared at her. At perfection. She was a little more casually dressed than usual in a blue-and-white-checked cotton blouse and blue jean shorts. His mother wouldn't have been caught dead in them since they came down almost to her knees. He liked them. Could stare at them and the person wearing them for hours, days, years.

If he were a different man.

"No, but if you didn't come back, I'm the one who would've had to do all the rescheduling."

Of course she would.

"Jane brought us back. She said if I didn't let her, she was calling you."

"You've been at the Miner's Lamp all this time?"

"We started out there, went to the park, finally took in a movie and then went to the Miner's Lamp again. There's not really much to do in town on a Sunday."

"Well, that was one of things I needed to tell you. I had time to check my emails today, and you've been added to our insurance. If you need to, and one's available, you can use a Lost Dutchman truck when you need to go to town."

"You trust me with a truck?"

She started to say "Ye..." then hesitated.

"Yes, no, which is it?"

"Yes, but, I was..." She stared at her hands. "I was worried that you wouldn't come back."

"I thought about it," he admitted. Then, he got annoyed at himself. He'd meant to have this conversation with her father. Jacob was his boss.

"I called my sister again," she admitted.

Great, more of his personal life scrutinized.

"And she told you I've got more problems than can be solved in one lifetime, right?" He didn't mean for the words to sound bitter, but he couldn't deny that he felt bitter. He kept trying to chase the feeling away, replace it with gratitude for what was going right, but the wrong was so much more prominent.

"That's not what she said."

"What did she say?"

"She said that Timmy's lucky to have someone willing to fight for him through one obstacle after another. She said most of her caseload would turn him over without a fight, be glad of it. She also said that it's not unusual to get out of prison and have trouble find you. She said it's part of a cycle that most aren't strong enough to battle."

Eva wasn't finished. "I'm sure glad you're strong."

He couldn't help it. He laughed. Strong? No one, in all his years, had called him strong. Not his mother, not a teacher, not a foster parent, certainly not anyone at the prison.

Eva stood, and Jesse thought she'd leave him in peace. After all, he'd just laughed at her. Instead she took his empty iced tea glass and refilled it, also getting one of her own.

When she came back, she said, "So, what are you going to do? Go or stay?"

"I didn't think going was an option."

"Harold told me he didn't expect you to return."

"Really? Well, I returned, didn't I?"

"For how long?"

"I don't know," he admitted.

The back door opened and Harold entered, as if he knew they were talking about him. He looked at the people playing UNO who were packing up. Then he looked at Jesse and Eva and frowned.

What was it he'd said on Jesse's first full day? Oh right, that Eva was a filly Jesse shouldn't get near. From his scowl, it was clear to see he hadn't changed his mind about that.

Before Jesse could stand, Eva waved the foreman over and said, "I told you Jesse would come back."

That's not what she'd confessed to Jesse just a few minutes ago. Then, she'd said she was worried.

She looked at Jesse and then back over at Harold before announcing, "I believe in him."

Jesse looked like he'd swallowed a cherry, whole. Harold pretty much had the same look.

She wanted her words back, wished she hadn't said them in front of Jesse. Now he had that look on his face. She'd seen it before, on her father. After her mother died, plenty of women came around, bearing casseroles and suggesting outings. He'd had the same expression on his face that Jesse did now—like he wished the ground would swallow him whole so he wouldn't have to deal with her and her expectations.

She'd just been so happy that Jesse had returned. Happy and confused. It bothered her how much she was drawn to him. He truly was not the type of man she should be reaching out to. He was taking her sights off the ranch, off her goals.

He was all wrong for her.

He reinforced that thought by standing, sending his chair scraping back. "Harold, good to see you. I'm going to go check on Timmy, check on the horses, and then get some sleep. Got a lot of work to do tomorrow. Night, Eva."

He strode across the floor before Eva could think of anything to say. Harold didn't give her time to regroup. "Eva, your dad's not real happy with Jesse right now."

"What happened? Do you know? One day Dad's saying he'll take Jesse to the rodeo, and the next he's saying maybe he'll see if one of his friends in Utah will hire Jesse on."

"That boy's got more problems than you can shake a stick at," Harold said. "Best you avoid him. I warned him to leave you a—"

Eva stood so fast she almost knocked her chair over. "Warned him to leave me alone? Why? Tell me one thing he's done that means you should warn him off me. One."

"If the fact that he's an ex-con doesn't warn you off, then there's the drunk the other night."

"Not Jesse's doing. Jesse didn't know the kid."

"So Jesse said. I'm not sure. Ex-cons have a way of reconnecting with old acquaintances and—"

"Harold, you know why I was so happy when

you walked into the dining hall, and why I called you over?"

"I—"

"I wanted you to talk to Jesse."

"About what? I talk to him all the time. For the past two weeks, I've pretty much taught him my job. Sometimes I feel like I'm training my replacement."

That surprised Eva. Quickly she reassured him, "You're irreplaceable."

"That's not true," he protested, though he looked pleased.

Eva sat back down. Leaning forward, she clasped Harold's hands in her own. "You know what I wanted you to talk about?"

"No, what?"

"I wanted you to tell him that you did five years on Rikers Island. I wanted you to tell him you came out a changed man, and that rehabilitation is possible."

"I'm not sure Jesse *is* a changed man. That drunk—"

"Think, Harold." Eva looked over at the UNO-playing family, now gathering their belongings. "Jesse has Timmy to consider. You've watching him go from one meeting to another, most because of his determination to do what's right for that little boy. Can you think of a better reason for a man to want to rehabilitate? And can you honestly say you haven't seen Jesse trying?"

"I do see him trying," Harold admitted. "But I also see all the clues that Jesse is trouble. Even if the drunk wasn't his fault, we've got the stolen car and the fact that somebody saw something and called Child Protective Services."

Her father walked in the dining hall. He looked like he always had, tall, strong and in charge.

"Wondered where you were," he said when he spotted Eva. "Harold, everything okay with the horses?"

"I put them to bed an hour ago. Jesse's checking on them now."

Jacob didn't even blink.

Eva wanted to burst out with "He came back, Dad," and "I told you he would," but she knew her father was having second thoughts about letting Jesse stay and didn't want to tip the scales. She'd never been one to hide her feelings. If she didn't want a new hand hired, she laid out the reasons why. If she wanted the pool updated, she left blueprints and photographs where her father could find them. If she was afraid to get on a horse, she backed out the door and let no one stop her. If she was falling in love, she stuck up for her man.

She didn't dare do that for Jesse. Didn't dare admit she was attracted to him because he didn't need any more roadblocks, and if Harold had warned Jesse off her, there was no telling what her father had done.

Would do.

Chapter Fifteen

Eva knew Jesse was avoiding her. Every morning he and Timmy ate breakfast lightning-fast and disappeared either before she got to the dining hall or as she was entering. She was pretty sure they were eating lunch and dinner at the booth in the kitchen with Cook. He took her phone calls with solemn efficiency, not allowing time for small talk.

She reminded herself that the ranch couldn't afford Jesse, that she'd tried to talk her dad out of hiring him, and that he continued to be more trouble than he was worth.

Maybe if she kept reminding herself, she'd eventually believe it. Instead, all she could think was that maybe Jesse's efforts to stay aloof for the past few days would convince her father that if he feared there was a romance developing between her and Jesse, there was nothing to worry about. Dad still was of the mindset, "Soon as he gets through this custody battle, he can start over in Utah."

Eva wanted her dad to go back to, "I think I'll take Jesse to the rodeo over in Payson. Show him the ropes" and "With your sisters off doing their own things and Harold getting slower, we need someone year-round."

Timmy, however, still showed up midmorning for his hose-down. If he noticed a difference in the way Jesse treated Eva, he wasn't saying. By day three, Eva knew to get her news from Cook, even though she really wanted to be asking Jesse these questions.

"The child psychologist said that Timmy has the ability to talk, just doesn't want to. She thinks he's afraid." Cook had willingly taken over the job of being Jesse's champion, which was funny because the last two times her father had taken in ex-cons, Cook had been afraid of them.

"What do they think Timmy's afraid of?"

"Not sure."

"Is he afraid because of something that happened in the past or afraid of something happening right now?"

"Not sure."

From Cook, Eva also found out that Jesse took Timmy to the pediatrician so there'd be a "before the call" to protective services report and an "after the call" report. Both visits reported a five-year-old boy who was a little underweight, who didn't talk and who needed glasses. Both visits documented no signs of bruises, broken bones or maltreatment.

"Jesse's losing money faster than a leaky boat."

"Is Jesse any closer to being Timmy's legal guardian?"

"He's still waiting for the DNA testing to come back. That'll take weeks. If not for the complaint to Child Protective Services, the lawyer would try to get Jesse officially registered as Timmy's foster father. That way, at least he could move forward with getting the boy in school and such."

Cook remembered something in the oven, and instead of following him, Eva headed outside to her favorite spot on the back porch. Jesse wasn't in sight. Harold was walking a limping horse into the barn. Man and horse walked alike. Already a few people were at the pool. One of the other summer wranglers and someone else—a guest?—were leaning against the back of the barn, out of Harold's sight. What were they doing?

Idiots. And the second man wasn't a guest. It was Mitch. And they were smoking cigarettes. That's all the Lost Dutchman needed: a fire.

Eva pulled out her cell phone and called her father. He was out on a group ride and didn't answer. Odd. He always took his phone. Next she tried Harold, but his hearing was so bad that he practically had to be holding the phone next to his ear in order to even notice the ringtone. Great, she'd need to go down there herself and confront Mitch.

Leaving the porch, she got her ATV and headed for the barn, parking by the entrance and jumping off before striding around the corner of the barn, hands on her hips. The smell of horses, heat and sweet grass followed her to the two miscreants.

One, a new hire this summer, had the sense to at least look guilty.

Mitch, on the other hand, gave her a slow grin as he put the cigarette out by pressing it against the toe of his boot.

"Howdy, Miss Hubrecht. You watching me from the porch again?"

"I wasn't watching you. I was watching the grounds. I just happened to see you. You know smoking's not allowed on the Lost Dutchman property. You signed a paper indicating you didn't smoke."

"I don't smoke often," Mitch said agreeably. "It's been a rough couple of weeks. We've been picking up the slack for Jesse, him taking his boy to so many doctors and appointments."

"Why wasn't it so rough three weeks ago, when we didn't have a third hand?" Eva asked. Using Jesse as an excuse was ludicrous. Both Mitch and the other wrangler had been here since May. Jesse hired on just this month. His being here made things easier, not harder.

"Things are kind of slow," Mitch said, clearly changing tactics. "Anything you need doing up at the main house?"

"Anything I need doing won't be done by a man smelling of cigarette smoke and stupid enough to smoke outside during dry conditions."

Mitch's eyes narrowed. Eva almost stepped back. She'd never been afraid of Mitch, but she'd never derided him that harshly before either. Her frayed nerves from the Jesse situation were making her harsher than she wanted to be. She usually was the kind of employer who didn't use the word *stupid*. Even if she thought it.

Mitch wasn't stupid, though—just lazy. He was the type of employee who knew what to do but often tried to get out of doing it. She shouldn't have phrased things that way, but she should and *would* make it clear to him that he needed to shape up.

"You're not wearing your uniform shirt," Eva said. "This isn't your day off."

"Both of mine are dirty."

"I'll get you one from storage." Bad enough he was out of uniform, but his bright orange shirt also advertised Rex's Bar and Grill.

She turned, took a few steps toward her ATV and stopped. This wasn't the first time she'd seen merchandise for Rex's Bar and Grill. The drunk who'd run over her father's foot had been wearing a hat from there. Bright orange was a beacon.

She swirled around, hands on her hips, and said, "Where is Rex's Bar and Grill?"

"In Congress, Arizona, where I'm from."

Congress was a small town, smaller even than Apache Creek. The odds of the drunk not knowing Mitch were slim to none.

Mitch, unaware that Eva was putting two and two together, said, "I'll take you there, some weekend when you get off. They usually have a nice band."

"I…" Eva struggled finding the words she wanted to say. She'd had years of treating people nicely, but this situation called for a rejection that could not be mistaken for anything else. "I think I'd rather rearrange my sock drawer."

The other wrangler laughed.

Mitch shot him a dirty look and said to Eva, "You'd rather be with the ex-con, right? Well, you deserve him. But I heard your daddy say he wouldn't be here long. *I'm* here. And, you're not getting any younger. It's time you start looking for a real man."

He puffed up a bit. The other wrangler had already sidled to the side of the barn. Now he disappeared altogether. Smart man.

"We can go into Phoenix some Monday night," Mitch continued. "Take in a movie, go out to eat, dancing after. I know some real good bars."

He'd been here two summers and hadn't caught

on to the fact that no alcohol was allowed on the premises, that neither she or her father condoned drinking?

"No."

"You can loosen up a little, wear some pretty clothes."

She looked down. Her royal-blue shirt advertised the Lost Dutchman, her jeans were clean and her tennis shoes didn't have holes in the toes. She was pretty enough, as far as she was concerned. It's not like she'd asked for Mitch's opinion. Before she could think of a comeback that would shut this conversation down, one that didn't utilize the word *stupid* but implied it, a horse turned the corner of the barn and moved the few feet to where she stood facing Mitch.

"Everything okay, Eva?" Jesse swung down from his horse. Behind him, Timmy did the same.

Two heroes.

"Mitch here is letting me know he's willing to help loosen me up. He also just put out a cigarette that he shouldn't have been smoking on this property in the first place. Oh, and read his shirt. It's advertising the same bar as the hat the drunk was wearing when he passed out and ran over Dad's toe."

At the end of a long afternoon, the other wrangler confessed that Mitch had called protective services because he wanted to be rid of Jesse, the sheriff confirmed that the drunk had listed a Congress address, and Mitch was fired.

Jesse was impressed with the way Jacob handled it. It all boiled down to disrespect to both the ranch and to Eva—mainly Eva. No one, Jacob had emphasized, treated Eva less than like a princess.

Jesse kept his mouth shut. He didn't think princesses needed to work as hard as Eva did, and he thought princesses should get listened to more.

Jesse couldn't claim he was sorry to see Mitch go, but there was an uneasy feeling in his gut that told him the young man leaving was too much like the old Jesse: lost and angry.

That thought stayed with Jesse as he drove to his Thursday night anger management class. At least now he knew why he needed these anger management classes. No, he had never been the violent type, but anger didn't always manifest itself outwardly. It could also simmer inwardly. Tonight, as if knowing something was amiss, the anger management instructor had put a scripture from Proverbs on the dry-erase board. "A hot-tempered man stirs up strife, but he who is slow to anger quiets contention." There'd been quite a few examples given—most from movies—in which holding one's temper worked for good.

"Glad it's not you leaving on the bus," Eva said later, when they were back in the Hubrechts' living room. It looked much the same as it had his last visit, except the cushions from the couch had been removed and made into a fort exactly the size of Timmy. Also, Eva's kachina doll was on an end table.

"I used her to talk him out of the fort and over here working with me." Eva again sat at her loom with Timmy beside her. She'd watched his son while Jesse attended his class. Timmy'd obviously had a good time. He was asleep next to Eva. His hand—the one with his favorite thumb for sucking—was entangled in some yarn. The blanket was already a good six inches longer than last time he'd been here.

"Did Timmy help you or hinder you?"

Eva hesitated. "For the most part, he helped and entertained. He's quite artistic, you know. He helped with colors and only had to be told once. But—" she pointed to the lower beam "—he accidentally stepped on this, and now there's a hairline crack. I'm going to need to load it up and take it to the rez. See if my uncle can repair it."

Jesse came closer and bent down. His son gently snored. He saw the crack, one that if left alone would weaken the structure. "I'm sorry."

"It was an accident. I know that. Right after he did it, he made the fort."

Jesse nodded. Then, moving to the big picture window, he stared at the panoramic view of cacti and desert and sand hills. Toward the back corner of the room was a table with a half-completed puzzle on it. This was new since last time. Jesse walked over and looked at the box.

"Dad does puzzles whenever he's upset. He's finished one and started that one since last Saturday."

"The day Ms. Comstocker showed up."

"The visit upset everyone," Eva agreed, "and I'm also pretty sure that Mitch said something to my dad that made him doubt you. That's why he's invited you here tonight. He wants to apologize."

"He could have done that in the barn."

"Dad doesn't apologize often. It's really been bothering him. Go easy on him. He's always prided himself on being a good judge of character even while taking in strays."

"Is that what I am, a stray?"

"No, Mitch was a stray. He's the son of one of Dad's old friends. Dad was hoping this place would give him some direction."

"Which is exactly why I'm here," Jesse said. "To find direction."

"You're here because Mike Hamm believes in you. We've known Mike fifteen years and only three other times has he asked us to take somebody on. You're not a stray, more a project."

"I'm not sure I like that any better."

"You told me you believe in honesty."

She had him there. And the silence that followed the words told him she expected honesty from him.

"I did more than steal a car," he said.

"I figured that."

"I turned eighteen in foster care. After that, I went into a group home, which I hated, so I took off. I slept on the streets for three nights, and then I met Matilda at a party. She'd just moved out on her own and needed a roommate. I moved in, I found a job working for a dry cleaner, and basically we drifted together doing just enough to get by."

"Sounds like a lot of young people I know," Eva pointed out.

"Not you."

"When my mother died, I had two little sisters. Dad and Patti were around, but when I hit thirteen, for some reason, my littlest sister Emily wouldn't let me out of her sight. She followed me the way Timmy follows you. Having a pint-size chaperone does a lot to keep one out of trouble." She left the loom, careful not to wake Timmy, and came to stand by Jesse at the picture window. The moon was a hazy orange. A few clouds, thin and transparent, slashed through the dusky sky.

"Timmy's the best thing that's ever happened to me. Those months with Matilda didn't make me a better person, but he will." Jesse paused only a moment before going on. "I met quite a few people through her. After she split, leaving me owing rent I couldn't afford, I moved in with some of her buddies."

"Did you call them when you were released, trying to find Matilda?"

"They're both still in prison. The three of us went in together." Jesse stepped away from the window, away from Eva. In some ways, he still felt like he didn't deserve the beauty that surrounded him.

Eva would have none of it. She stepped away from the window, too. "I hope someone like Mike helps them. Why are they still in and you're out?"

"It was a Friday night. We were bored and broke and stupid. Billy jumped up and said he had to get out of the apartment, that he couldn't stand its walls anymore. Neither could we. Steve and I followed him. I still remember how impressed I was that he could hotwire a car. He'd done it a couple of times, but we'd only taken those cars for joyrides, left them in good shape. This time, though, I got behind the wheel, and Billy told me to stop at the convenience store at the end of town."

"You thought he'd found some money?"

"No, I knew he was going in to steal something. He had his backpack. We'd done this before. One of us would be the decoy, distract the clerk. The other would steal some beer. It's petty theft, not a big crime. That's what I thought back then."

"But you wound up serving time."

"Because this time the clerk noticed what was happening. He came from behind the counter and went after Billy. Steve panicked as they were heading for the door and hit him over the head with a bottle. I think it was reaction more than intent. The clerk went down. I saw the blood start to pool. Billy and Steve came barreling out and jumped in the car."

"You left?" He had to give her credit. She didn't step away.

"No. I jumped out of the car and ran to the store. I took off my shirt and tied it around his head. Then I called nine-one-one. Billy and Steve took off."

"Did—did the clerk die?"

"No, but it was a head wound, so it bled like crazy. I think he got like sixteen stitches. They arrested Billy, Steve and me on grand theft auto and robbery. The minute Steve caused bodily harm to the clerk, our crime went from theft to robbery. The only reason I served less time was that there were witness testimonies and security tape footage to show that I left the car and ran to help."

"I'm glad you did."

"It didn't occur to me not to."

"Because even before you found God, that's the kind of person you were."

"I wish I were the kind of person who'd have

found a job, found friends with jobs and stayed out of trouble."

"Everyone gets in at least a little trouble. Some just find bigger trouble than others. Luckily for me and my sisters, Dad kept a pretty tight rein. Kept all of us girls out of real trouble."

"You have a great family," Jesse said.

"I do. Not perfect, but great. I remember one night Dad came and fetched me from a party that was starting to get out of control. How he knew, he never said. One minute I was leaning against the wall and somebody was handing me a beer and I was going to take it. The next, Dad was handing the beer back to the kid and guiding me to the door. I was so embarrassed. As we were leaving, Dad was throwing statements over his shoulder like 'Jane, your mom's working the early shift tomorrow' and 'Sam, see you in church on Sunday.'"

"My mother would have taken a beer for herself and pretended she was my friend instead of my mother."

"You won't be that kind of father," Eva pointed out.

"No, I won't." Jesse smiled as he looked across at her. She was as tall as he was. He could look right into those deep brown eyes.

She smiled back. "By the way, you're Dad's project, not mine. In the beginning, I didn't want you here at all."

He'd overheard enough to know that already.

"If it makes you feel any better—" Eva stopped weaving, looked up and met his gaze "—I want you here now."

"Ahem."

Jesse turned, and Eva went back to weaving. Jacob remained in the doorway. "I didn't realize you were already here," he said to Jesse.

"I was admiring your puzzle." It was partly true, and Jesse didn't think the time was right to admit that he was also admiring Jacob's daughter.

For the next twenty minutes, Jacob and he connected a dozen pieces and sorted a dozen more, and Jesse was offered a full-time position and a raise.

"That's how my dad apologizes," Eva said later, as she walked him and a still half-asleep Timmy from the room. "Are you going to accept?"

"I don't know. Jacob's going to call Ms. Comstocker tomorrow morning and tell her what he's learned. I'll tell my parole officer and the lawyer. I need them to believe in me."

"I believe in you."

He didn't respond, because the only thing he wanted to do right then was lean forward, take her face in his hands and kiss her. He was bothered not only by how much he wanted to but also by the fact that as they stood there, he was starting to lean toward her.

And she was leaning toward him.

Taking Timmy by the hand, he angled the boy so he was between them. "I'll see you in the morning," Jesse said, starting to move down the steps.

"Good, no more hurrying so you don't have to face me."

"Safer that way," Jesse insisted gently. He guided Timmy down the remaining steps, and together they started walking down to the barn. Tonight had taught Jesse many things. Mainly that running from your troubles never paid off. He'd also learned that the chemistry between him and Eva wasn't going unnoticed.

He wondered just how much Eva's dad had witnessed tonight before clearing his throat.

Mitch had noticed it and tried to end it. First by telling Jacob a few untruths and then by calling Child Protective Services.

"I'll have to forgive him," Jesse said aloud.

Timmy didn't answer.

Jesse went on. "What Mitch did wasn't kind. It was mean. It hurt people. It hurt us. But if I allow the anger to boil inside, then it might take over, change me, make me unhappy."

Timmy nodded.

"You understand?" Jesse was a bit surprised. In all the yes/no questions he'd gotten used to asking his son, he'd never gotten deep. "Are you angry at someone?"

Timmy nodded.

"Are you angry at Matilda? At your mother?"

Timmy didn't nod. He went to his knees, grabbing at the dirt under his feet and keening. Behind them, the porch light came on, and Eva and her father stepped out. Jesse held up a hand, halting them.

"It's okay," Jesse said. "It's okay for you to be sad, to cry. Throw the dirt if you have to. It's not right for people to do things that hurt us. But maybe your mother had a reason for leaving you with me. And, Timmy, I gotta tell you. You're the best thing that's ever happened to me."

He heard a sound behind him and turned to see Eva holding on to the back porch railing. Tears streamed from her eyes. Jesse didn't dare tell her that she was another amazing thing that had happened to him. Right now, his son was more important. Gathering Timmy up, he took one step and then another. At first, Timmy flailed a bit, and hot tears dampened Jesse's cheeks—tears shed by both Timmy and him.

When they got to the barn, Jesse set Timmy down. Going to his knees, Jesse looked Timmy in the eyes. "I will tell you this every day for the rest of your life, even if I had to shout it to the wind and hope you hear it.

"I love you."

Chapter Sixteen

Friday morning, Jesse saddled nine horses. With Mitch gone, there were fewer people to do the work. Jacob saddled three horses himself, not once complaining about how his toe felt in his boot.

The ride was one of the better ones. They had a few townies; the rest were guests—families, doing things together.

Jesse watched, noting the interplay between fathers and sons. One family had an eighteen-year-old. He was heading off to college, Princeton no less, come August. He was a man more than a child, but the father still gave suggestions, still wanted to prevent the son, who was bigger than he was, from falling should the horse stumble.

The other family had twin daughters. They chattered and giggled the whole ride. Their mother chattered and giggled with them. The father rolled his eyes good-naturedly.

It was the end of July, still hot but not as hot as the day Jesse was released. The transparent clouds had grown in size and changed texture. Jacob predicted a monsoon. Timmy increased the space he was willing to put between him and Jesse. Sometimes a half hour would go by before Jesse would fetch Timmy from working with Eva, either at the front desk or at her loom. Twice Timmy had gone off on a ride with Jacob, leaving Jesse behind.

Jesse saw Eva often. They ate breakfast together, sometimes lunch. At the end of the evening, they met in the dining hall and taught Timmy to play UNO. Timmy hit the table three times when he was down to one card. When Timmy fell asleep, Eva helped Jesse with financial planning. There wasn't much to plan with. Timmy's pediatrician had already taken a third of Jesse's earnings. The lawyer was pro bono; his investigator was not. No matter how many ways Eva and Jesse worked it, he wasn't making enough to pay his bills.

"Now that you're full-time, you'll get insurance," Eva said. "For you and Timmy—so his doctor's bills will be covered, at least." To Jesse's way of thinking, it couldn't happen fast enough.

Sunday, at church, they sat together. After church, Crystal Glenn mentioned that she would no longer need riding lessons.

Monday morning, Timmy got up and took a shower. Jesse almost wished he had a camera.

His boy knew how to take a shower! Most men were proud of baseball hits, a perfect spelling test and such. Not Jesse. His kid knew how to take a shower! He called Eva and asked her to meet him downstairs.

Timmy walked in front of him, hair still wet. Jesse felt his grin, so wide it hurt. Eva didn't even need prompting.

"Timmy, you look wonderful!"

He nodded.

"And you," Jesse said, getting an idea, "are standing in a barn, surrounded by horses, and you're not even breathing heavily."

She rolled her eyes. "I'm a good five feet from a horse. I can take this."

"Timmy, you take one of Eva's hands and I'll take the other."

Timmy moved quickly, his grin mirroring his father's. He took Eva's left hand while Jesse took her right. She laughed a bit, but Jesse heard the faint nervousness.

"Never show fear," he whispered. "Horses are smart. They sense how a person feels. They judge. You have to prove them wrong."

Palomino Pete snorted, as if he knew Jesse was feeding Eva a line.

"You're going to be fine," Jesse said. "All we're going to do is pet Palomino Pete. He likes a little attention in the morning. Never mind that he's already a little hot and sweaty. If you're going to get back in the saddle, you're going to do it the cowgirl way."

Eva swatted away a fly. Palomino Pete stepped back. Jesse said to Timmy, "Go get one of the carrots Jacob keeps stashed in the saddle room."

Timmy took off, leaving Jesse and Eva alone.

Jesse took Eva's hand. He held it up so he could look at it. "Strong," he murmured. There were other things he noted. She favored clear nail polish, and her fingers were warm as they clasped his. "A hand this strong can handle a horse. No problem."

He rubbed his thumb against the palm of her hand. "A hand this strong could handle anything, anyone."

"Like you," she whispered.

Luckily, Timmy walked in before Jesse could answer. Maybe it was the lead-up, maybe it was the company, but when Jacob entered the barn a moment later, he stopped, watching as his oldest daughter fawned over Palomino Pete.

"Good work," he told Jesse. "Now, saddle up twelve horses. We've got a trail ride in an hour."

That afternoon, he and Timmy drove into town to see Jesse's parole officer. It was an easy visit. Afterward, they went to see the lawyer, which was not so easy.

"Still no word on Matilda Scott's whereabouts."

That was the bad news. The good news was Officer Sam Miller had taken it upon himself to contact Ms. Comstocker. Consequently, Jesse's petition to foster was under consideration.

It was enough.

It was midafternoon when he got back to the Lost Dutchman. He had no tasks and a couple of hours to himself. He and Timmy headed for one of sheds out back. It took him only a few minutes to gather what he needed. Timmy carried the pieces of wood. Jesse handled the tools and steel. First stop was Jacob's workshop.

"We're going to make a temporary beam protector," Jesse said. "We'll make it out of steel, but cover it with wood so it matches the rest of the loom. It'll look a little bigger on one side, but when Eva gets it to her uncle, he can remove it and repair it professionally."

Jesse and Timmy worked together for two hours. Jesse handled the cutting and gluing. Timmy was a mean sander. Later, Patti let them into the living room where Jesse, using a glue that could later be easily removed with heat, repaired Eva's loom so it wouldn't crack any further.

"You go get her," Jesse told Timmy. "Bring her here."

When Eva came in the room, she had her eyes closed, and Timmy was leading her. She opened them, and Jesse was standing next to the portion of the loom he'd just repaired.

"Ohhhh" was all she said. She came to the loom, running her hand along the heddle, the shuttle and finally the beam. "It's perfect."

Jesse bent down, motioning her to follow. "When you get it to your uncle, just use a hair dryer and you can remove this portion—"

"What? It's repaired. I'm fine with it exactly like this." She proceeded to show him other areas of the loom that had been repaired over the years. Some, exactly the way he'd repaired it.

"There's nothing broken that cannot be made whole," she said.

He got the idea she was talking about more than the loom.

Her cell phone sounded, ruining the moment. She looked at the screen and ignored the call. Coming around the loom, she bent. To Jesse's surprise, Timmy walked into her arms and allowed a hug.

The moment was almost perfect. Then, Eva looked at the fireplace and said, "Where's my kachina?"

Jacob was of a mind that a guest had taken it. Eva didn't agree. If a guest had taken it, they'd have taken all three. They weren't that heavy, and they'd fit in suitcases. The entire main house was searched.

Cook was a bit indignant when they got to the kitchen, but then pitched in to help when he saw the look on Eva's face.

Eva didn't assist with supper that night. She couldn't. Instead, she sat at her loom and started weaving. The space on top of the fireplace shelf glared at her. Where could the kachina be? She'd taken it down last Thursday when Timmy was with her. But she'd returned it to its rightful spot. It had been there last night.

Jacob stuck his head through the living room doorway. He'd been walking on tiptoes since the doll went missing. "I called Sam Miller. There's an accident out near the interstate, but he says he'll come by in the morning and take an official report."

"We don't even have a picture," Eva mourned. She buried herself in her weaving, remembering her mother's hands on hers, guiding her ever so gently: in, out, over, under. Never did her mother raise her voice.

The orange moon was back, with it the thin clouds. Her father's predicted monsoon hadn't occurred. Instead, a different storm had struck.

She heard the knock just as the clock struck nine and knew who was at the door. "Come in," she called.

Jesse stepped into the room. "I missed you at supper." His words were simple; the expression on his face was not. "Jacob said you wanted to be alone. I put Timmy to sleep and thought I'd come check on you. But I'll leave if you want me to."

Eva wasn't sure what she wanted. In some ways, it felt like she'd lost her mother again. But really, the kachina was just a thing, a thing!

She felt the tears pool in her eyes and wiped them before they could fall. Jesse came and sat behind her. Wrapping her in his arms, he rocked her back and forth, until she let her head drop. She'd never had anyone invade her space so. Who was this man who made her feel so safe?

"Some people," she said, "believe the kachina is a messenger. When I was eight, after my mother died, the kachina was in my bedroom. I kept it on the nightstand. Sometimes I even put it in bed with me. I pretended it was my mother and I'd talk to it. I'd even pretend it answered."

"We'll find it."

"Don't even try to make me one," she joked, choking a little.

"Don't worry. I know my limitations."

They sat together, his arms around her, she holding one of his hands, until the grandfather clock struck ten and it was time for bed.

Tuesday the clouds were back. A record number of guests stood in line for a July ride. Jesse and Harold went on the first outing. When they got back, Jacob was already prepping for the next.

"What if it storms?" Jesse asked.

"We'll know and we'll turn back. This group is a family of five, all experienced riders. I've taken them out a hundred times. They called this morning. This kind of business keeps up, Eva can talk me into updating the pool."

Jesse no more than washed his face and hands before he was out on the second ride. This time, Timmy was awake and riding along, looking all the while at the sky.

"This will be a short ride," Jesse promised.

And it was. But only for Jesse and Timmy. Ten minutes in, the sound of an approaching horse came from behind. Eva, looking both terrified and determined, trotted up beside Jesse.

"You're riding!" He wanted to jump down from his horse, pull her into his arms, and give her the kind of kiss…

The kind of kiss he wasn't willing to give in full view of her father.

"Why are you riding?"

"The ATV wouldn't start. Then, I couldn't find Harold, and I didn't trust anyone else. Oh, Jesse, you've gotta come back, now." Eva looked at Timmy, and Jesse couldn't quite read her expression.

"Ms. Comstocker's back!" Jesse guessed. He

heard the panic in his voice and saw Timmy's face go from a big smile to blank.

That exasperating blank look.

"It's not Ms. Comstocker." Eva was breathing heavily. She had one hand locked around the saddle horn as if it was glued there. At least her other hand held the reins correctly. "It's worse."

What could be worse? Jesse pulled on the reins. Snow White came to a halt. Pinocchio followed suit. Palomino Pete stopped, too, moving his head restlessly, letting Eva know she needed to give a bit more rein.

Eva quickly said, "She arrived about twenty minutes ago. Sam Miller pulled in right behind her. He's arresting her, Jesse."

"Who?" Jesse couldn't figure out what had Eva all flustered. Who could be worse than Ms. Comstocker?

"It's Matilda."

A rumble came from the distance as Jesse wheeled Snow White around. One of the horses pranced to the left, its rider gasping a bit but not losing control. Everyone looked at the sky.

"You bring Timmy," Jesse told Jacob. "I want to speak to Matilda alone first."

Eva said, "I'll watch Timmy and stay with Dad, make sure everything's okay."

They hadn't been that far out, but the ride back to the Lost Dutchman seemed to take forever. When Jesse got close to the barn, he saw the unfamiliar car blocking the entrance and the police cruiser next to it. Matilda Scott was slumped against the rusted Volkswagen. Her red hair looked like it hadn't been combed in a week. Her head was nodding forward as if she couldn't stay awake.

Above, gray clouds swirled, the skies matching his mood.

Sam Miller hurried toward Jesse. "Mr. Campbell, I came out here to take a report for Eva's missing kachina. I watched this car driving up the road, weaving a little. When she pulled in and parked, I followed. I thought I was just going to arrest another drunk. I managed to get her identification. The minute I said her name, Eva was off like a shot."

"I don't want you to arrest her. She's Timmy's mother. I'll take care of this." From the corner of his eyes, he saw the horses returning.

"It's out of your hands," Sam said. "I knocked on the window to get her attention. She opened the door and fell out."

"That's not a crime, unless she's drunk. Are you arresting her for drunk driving?"

"Yes, but there's more." Sam looked at Matilda's

feet. She grinned at Jesse when he looked, too. The baggy was half under her foot and half spilling out.

"Cocaine?"

"Yes. We're talking both driving under the influence and—" Sam paused as Eva and Timmy rode up, both dismounting their horses right behind him "—we're talking possession. Also, we're probably looking at another stolen vehicle."

"I'll go to the station with you."

A tiny body came barreling across the way. Timmy skidded to a stop, pulled on his arm and nodded vigorously.

"No," Jesse said, "you can stay with Eva. This might take some time."

Timmy looked at Matilda, who tried to hold her head up but couldn't. Just like that, Timmy left Jesse's side and ran to her, grabbing her around the waist, and started crying. Not the keening he usually did, but the kind of real sobs a broken little boy was supposed to utter.

Jesse didn't know what to do. Looking at Eva, who'd joined them, he held up his hands. "This is beyond me."

"Take him with you," she advised. "And explain to him what's going on. So far, being honest with him has worked the best."

"Okay," Jesse said. "Come on, Timmy. We're going upstairs so I can get my wallet. Then we'll follow Officer Miller to the police station. We'll make sure Matilda, your mommy, is taken care of. That okay with you, Officer Miller?"

"Fine with me."

"I'll come, too." Eva wasn't offering; she was telling.

"Looks like I'll be unsaddling a whole lot of horses by myself," Jacob said. "Okay by me. You guys get this taken care of."

Jesse hurried into the barn and up the stairs two at a time. Timmy didn't follow. He was still holding on to his mother. Jesse couldn't hear the words, but Eva was saying something. No doubt trying to urge Timmy away from Matilda.

The apartment was in various stages of disarray. Jesse's room was clean, but his wallet wasn't there. The kitchen table was covered in drawings and crayons. As for the living room, it was half fort, half furniture. Jesse's wallet was on the coffee table. He bent to retrieve it, just happening to glance at Timmy's fort.

A wrapper of half-eaten crackers was on a blanket. One edge of the blanket was bulky, covering something Timmy had stowed under it. Jesse could make out a round section of wooden base.

A day that couldn't get much worse did. Reaching down, Jesse pulled what was hidden from under Timmy's blanket. At that moment, Officer

Miller came in the door saying, "Hey, if you have any of the paperwork…"

Jesse turned, looking the policeman full in the face.

"I'll take that," Officer Miller said.

Jesse handed over Eva's kachina.

Chapter Seventeen

Eva wasn't sure she wanted to know what was happening. Sam had hurried after Jesse, muttering something about paperwork. Next thing she knew, Sam was escorting Jesse from upstairs. He'd opened the back door of his cruiser, cupped the top of Jesse's head, and helped Jesse into the back seat next to Matilda.

Timmy tugged on Eva's shirt and pointed.

"I know. I know," Eva said.

"Eva," Sam said. "I'm sorry. I went up to see if Jesse had any paperwork he wanted us to mention when we interrogated Matilda. The door to the apartment was open. I caught him standing in the middle of the living room holding this." Sam held up Eva's kachina.

Eva opened her mouth. She wanted to say, "Jesse didn't take that." But she didn't. What other explanation was there? Mitch wasn't here anymore, and no one else would have put her doll in Jesse's apartment.

"I didn't take the doll," Jesse said. "It was in the apartment, with—"

"You can tell me the whole story downtown," Sam said. "Also, I'll call Child Protective Services. I know someone is already assigned to Timmy's case."

"No." Eva wasn't about to let Timmy suffer because of a choice his father had made. She'd known Jesse needed money. What she hadn't known was how badly he wanted it—how far he'd go to get it. Or, what a good actor he was. "I no longer consider it stolen. I take back the charges."

Sam just looked at her.

She changed tactics. "Timmy can stay here. I'll apply to be his foster parent. Dad will help."

"Just one minute," Jesse started. "I—" Sam closed the cruiser down and shrugged. "I'm not sure how it works. I'll still have to call Child Protective Services, but I'll tell them the boy is in a safe environment with people he knows and trusts."

Timmy squawked. He took one giant step toward the cruiser, and Eva barely caught him. She hugged him tightly, surprised by how strong he was. "It's okay, Timmy. I'll take you to visit him. I promise. And you know I keep my promises.

Right now he's in a bit of trouble. I'm not sure what's going to happen."

"And, Eva," Sam continued, "I'm sorry, but I've got to take the doll as evidence."

"Okay." Eva was too shocked to argue. Sam got in the cruiser, said something into his radio, and backed up to turn the car around. Timmy struggled like crazy until Jacob came and stood by him and said, "Timmy, you're not helping your dad by acting this way."

"Dad's right," Eva said. "Remember how your dad asked you to help when Ms. Comstocker came? You sat by him on the couch. He was so proud."

Timmy stilled, but Eva could feel him trembling.

"I'm surprised," Jacob said. "I believed Jesse had really turned his life around. I thought for sure this one was willing to change his ways. I'm shocked that he stole your kachina."

"I told him it was priceless," Eva said softly. "And he needs money."

The cruiser drove by them. Matilda looked like she was singing. Jesse's head was bowed.

Bowed in prayer.

Something Eva had forgotten to do.

She'd been too busy believing the worst.

Oh, Father, what have I done? Forgive me. The kachina's just a thing, a thing.

She'd told herself that once before. And Jesse Campbell had entered the living room and rocked her.

Rocked her world.

She should have given him the kachina, told him to sell it and take Timmy to every specialist out there.

As if knowing she was thinking about him, Timmy tugged on her shirt.

"Let's go, Timmy," Eva said. "Let's get to the station and see about getting your dad released. It's my kachina, and I'll say he didn't steal it."

"I did," Timmy whispered.

"What?" Eva wasn't sure she'd heard correctly, heard at all.

"I took your doll. I wanted it to talk to me like it used to talk to you."

"Oh, my." Eva's breathing came in short spurts. She didn't know what she was happier about: Timmy talking or hearing that Jesse had nothing to do with the doll going missing.

Wait! She'd known. Deep in her heart she'd known. Now, she had to hope that Jesse would forgive her for doubting him for even a second.

Dropping to her knees, she hugged Timmy. "That's all we need to know. Thank you for being honest with me. Come on, Timmy. We're going chase down that cop car and get your dad. He's gonna cry when he hears you speak. I'm so glad I'll get to be part of it."

Even though Timmy's legs were shorter, he kept up with Eva as she ran into the lobby, grabbed a set of keys and headed for one of the trucks. He'd just gotten his seat belt clipped when she started the engine. A half mile from the Lost Dutchman, they caught up with Sam Miller's cruiser. Eva honked. It took a moment, but Sam pulled over.

Both Eva and Timmy scrambled out of the driver's side door. Sam exited the cruiser. Eva had Timmy by the hand and dragged him over until they almost stumbled against Sam. At that moment, the monsoon her dad had been predicting sent a gust of wind, dragging Eva's hair in her face and forcing her to shout. "Jesse didn't do it. Tell him, Timmy. Tell him."

"I took the doll. I hid it in my fort."

In the cruiser, Matilda had stopped singing. Her eyes were bright, and she wasn't moving. Jesse, however, was leaning forward, staring out the window at Timmy and Eva.

"Oh, Sam, let him out. You heard Timmy. He needed it. He didn't realize he was stealing. It's my doll, and I say it wasn't theft. And anyway, Jesse was not involved."

"You sure?" Sam asked.

"I've never been so sure about anything. We never got around to filling out a report, you know."

"That's true," Sam said slowly, walking over to Jesse's side of the vehicle and opening the door. As Jesse burst from the cruiser, Sam continued, "I still need Jesse down at the station. He'll have to answer a few questions about Matilda."

Nobody really heard him.

Jesse was at Timmy's side in a dozen steps. Lifting the boy in the air, he twirled around and turned to face Matilda. Loud enough to be heard through the window glass, he announced. "This is my son!"

She nodded.

Eva leaned forward and whispered, "This isn't the place to do this. You'll want to ask these questions, get these answers, in front of the right authorities. You'll want all this documented."

Sam went back to the driver's side of the car and opened the door to climb in. "You two head down to the station. Ideally, I won't keep you there long." Eva nodded her understanding, and Sam drove away, leaving Jesse, Timmy and Eva standing alone by the street.

Jesse set Timmy down and, to Eva's surprise, drew her to his side. He felt strong, solid, upright.

"I was praying, you know," he said. "And God answered every prayer. Matilda's here, and we'll prove Jesse's my son. In the cruiser, I wasn't even praying that Jesse would talk—at least, I hadn't gotten around to it yet—and look! God answered that prayer, too. Then, you came after me?"

"I realized you hadn't stolen my kachina the moment Sam turned from the driveway, and even before Timmy tugged on my shirt and said his first words."

"Wish I could have heard them."

"You're going to be hearing his words for a long time to come. Just wait." Eva looked up, noticing the clouds darkening, the rain starting to fall. Without separating them, she nudged him toward the truck.

Then the sky opened, and the rain fell hard. Timmy struggled out of his dad's arms and ran toward the truck, scrambling in and settling in the middle. Eva made a move to follow, but Jesse grabbed her by the hand and brought her back to him, holding her tightly against him.

"You came after me," he repeated.

"I've told you more than once," she said coyly. "I believe in you."

He tilted her chin with one finger, until her lips were right in front of his. "How long will you believe?" he asked.

"I'll believe forever," she answered.

This time, he kissed her. There was no almost, no this-shouldn't-be-happening, no hesitation.

"Good," he said, once they'd kissed long enough to be thoroughly soaked. "Because I've just figured out the scripture that belongs to you and me."

"Scripture?" Eva couldn't believe he'd come up

with a scripture while they stood on the side of the road, in the rain, and on their way to the police station.

"It's John 14:16. It says, 'And I will ask the Father and he will give you another advocate to help you and be with you forever.' I finally get it.

"No," he added a moment later, correcting himself. "I finally got it, got you."

"Forever," she agreed, kissing him again.

* * * * *

Dear Reader,

Welcome to the Lost Dutchman Ranch! It's mostly a mishmash of places I've been and a world I used to dream would be mine. Yup, I was one of those girls with plastic horses in her bedroom, and my favorite books were from the *Gypsy* series written by Sharon Wagner.

A while ago, my family and I went on vacation, and we spent part of a day on horseback. I'd not ridden in almost fifteen years! As we traversed the trail, I realized I was *scared.* For some reason, the horse was a lot taller than I remembered. He also stumbled a bit more than I expected. What if I fell?

The heroine in *Finally a Hero* lives on a dude ranch. Her whole family is about horses. And she's afraid of them. It affects everything she does.

The hero didn't grow up with horses, but he's a natural with them. It's everything else in life that he can't seem to control.

I hope you enjoy reading *Finally a Hero* as much as I enjoyed writing it. It contains so much of what I love about Arizona. Our heroine Eva Hubrecht is half Hopi Indian, and with that heritage comes a wealth of history. The setting of *Finally a Hero* is a town called Apache Creek. I patterned it after the beautiful Apache Junction area, where the Superstition Mountains have fables that follow after you and tap you on the shoulder, whispering, "There's gold in them there hills."

For all that, *Finally a Hero* is the hero's journey. Jesse Campbell has a past that brought him to his knees. Good thing, because that's an awesome position for prayer.

I love hearing from my readers. Feel free to visit my website, www.pamelatracy.com. Oh, and don't forget to look for Eva's sisters and their stories… coming soon!

Pamela Tracy